Scream

A Lakeview Novel

STACEY R. CAMPBELL

green darner PRESS

Scream

A Lakeview Novel

green darner PRESS

Published by Green Darner Press
9600 Stone Avenue North
Seattle, Washington 98103

Green Darner Press is an imprint of Gemelli Press LLC

Cover design and typesetting by Enterline Design Services LLC

ISBN: 978-0-9864390-0-1
Library of Congress Control Number: 2015947014

To Halle
My Muse

AUTHOR'S NOTE

I have changed the character of "Uncle Mark" in *Hush* to "Uncle Mike," to reflect the name of the real police detective for whom he was named.

CHAPTER 1

Miami, Florida

The stiff brim of his Florida Gators hat did little to block the sun. The alarm on his phone sounded for the third time. The men he was supposed to meet were late.

Parked out of sight between two empty buildings, Ramon stood next to the car, his fists jammed into the pockets of his double-extra-large cargo shorts. He hated this part of the job. Jumpy buyers were bad for business. Sweat dripped from his hairline and rivered down the center of his back. What showed of his short, military-style brown hair glistened in the sun. In the trunk of his '67 Impala sat the biggest stash of drugs he had ever tried to sell at one time, over $1.5 million in cocaine. If the deal went down like he hoped, he'd never have to sell again.

His wife, Lola, strummed her long, freshly painted fuchsia nails against the deep-red vinyl dash. Her hair was beginning to frizz. If the deal didn't go down soon there would be hell to pay when they got home for making her wait so long. A Cuban rumba played through the new Pioneer speakers he just had installed in the car.

Both Lola and Ramon had lived in the same three-mile radius of Miami their whole lives, their families poor but prominent members of the Latino community, having made their way to America from Cuba several years after the revolution in the mid-1960s. America, however, never fulfilled its promise of prosperity, leaving Ramon and Lola wanting more.

"Can you stop that?" Ramon barked. "You'll scratch the vinyl."

Lola wanted the picket fence, the two point five children, and the goddamn dog. Not the trailer parked next to the tracks, where they currently lived. But after today Ramon would be able to step up to the plate, make it all happen, and finally give Lola the life she deserved.

Ramon's cell phone rang. "Yeah?"

"They're here," Nico said.

Nico Soto, Ramon's partner, sat on the other side of the abandoned mill. When he phoned, Ramon would grab the sample they'd put together and meet him. If the dealers liked what they saw, Lola would bring the Impala over and they'd make the deal.

"Good." Ramon shoved the barrel of his Smith and Wesson .44 Magnum into his waistband and untucked his T-shirt. He liked that it was the same kind of gun Clint Eastwood used in *Dirty Harry*. They didn't make movies like that anymore. The weight of the cold steel against his skin made him feel like a badass.

He banged three times on the roof of the car. "This is it, babe."

Lola snapped her gum and slid into the driver's seat. Ramon glanced back at her, tipping his chin.

Lola ran a hand down the wheel and started the engine.

CHAPTER 2

West Vancouver–Nanaimo ferry

British Columbia, Canada

Six years later

Late afternoon sun flooded the ferry's busy passenger deck. Halle could barely see the rocky coastline passing by through the salt-streaked glass. She closed her eyes, sighing, letting the sunlight dance over her lids and eyelashes. Long weekends away from campus always passed too quickly.

"Hey, I'm going to get something to eat. You want anything?" Halle's boyfriend, Alex, asked, sitting next to her.

"No, thanks. I'm good."

Alex brushed his lips against Halle's cheek in a soft kiss, making her smile. "How about you, Iz?" he said to his sister.

Focused on her phone, Izzy waved off her twin brother with one hand while continuing to text with the other, her multiple metal bracelets clinking together as if warning him not to interrupt her again.

"I'm surprised she hasn't worn out her screen," Alex whispered. Halle giggled.

"I can hear you," Izzy smirked. "Just because you don't appreciate good gossip doesn't mean you can be rude."

Leaning over, Alex covered Halle's lips with his own and pulled her onto his lap. He wove his fingers through her long golden-brown hair. He loved her hair. He wrapped a strand around his finger, playing with it. The top four buttons of her oversized plaid shirt gaped, revealing Alex's favorite T-shirt, which she wore with leggings and black lace-up, combat-style boots.

"Hey, what's this?" he teased, fingering the coarse dark green ribbing along the neck.

Heat rose in Halle's cheeks. "Nothing."

"Nuh-uh. That's mine, you little klepto."

"Finders keepers."

Glancing up, Izzy rolled her eyes. "God, you guys, get a room."

Halle and Alex met almost five years ago, on her first day as a student at Lakeview Academy. Because Alex was her roommate's brother, they'd skated around their attraction to one another until their grade 10 year. Now, as grade 12s, they held the record for the longest relationship on campus.

She still remembered the first time she saw him. He came walking into her room before she'd even met Izzy. He said hi and Halle, at just thirteen, didn't know what to think, but her heartbeat skipped and still did every time he looked at her with those big blue eyes. Izzy had them too, the eyes. Halle would have called the color sky blue, but that didn't seem to do them justice. They were more the color of the robin's eggs you find in the woods when hiking in the spring. Alex, once tall and thin, had filled out over the years. Rowing for their school's team had broadened his shoulders and turned his torso into a magazine-worthy washboard.

Halle, too, had grown. Gone were her braces and insecurities. Now, she was the second tallest in her class, not quite five feet eleven, but close. Izzy, however, remained as petite as the day they met, still pushing five feet two, although her attitude more than made up for her lack of inches. Halle could remember begging her parents to allow her to dye a strip of her hair the same color as Izzy's hot-pink stripe during their first year together. They said no, but Halle would never forget how cool the vivid color looked against Izzy's dark Mediterranean skin and almost-black hair.

Halle's shoulders tensed as she felt Alex's breath ease over the sensitive skin below her ear. "Stop," she warned, pushing him away. "That tickles."

Alex buried his nose in her hair. "Make me."

CHAPTER 3

"Sure you don't want anything?" Alex asked, letting Halle slip from his legs back onto the bench next to him.

After dating for over two years, Alex still couldn't get enough of her. He wished the school gave them more than just a couple of days off at the end of winter term. He loved spending time with her outside the strict confines of dorm life, where they were barely allowed to kiss in public without being harassed by the teachers. Halle usually joined their family during the shorter school breaks, when it wasn't feasible for her to fly home to Europe. This time, however, he and Iz had gone with Halle to the mainland, to visit her aunt and uncle. They lived in a small town just north of West Vancouver.

Halle used to live closer to the school, in the small town of Anacortes, Washington, located not too far from the Canadian border where her adoptive parents, Graham and Lili Henry, had raised Halle and her sister. That changed, however, when her sister, Blakely, discovered her biological family had been royalty and that she was the only living heir to the throne of the small Mediterranean country of Tamura. The truth of Blakely's unique situation became public when Blakely was in grade 12 at Lakeview Academy, the year before Alex and Izzy started there. Now, Blakely's ascent from normal teenager to teen queen seemed like old news, and Halle was able to lead a relatively normal life. considering she lived in a castle halfway around the world when she was not at Lakeview.

A noise like a low roll of thunder filled the air, and Halle glanced at Alex's stomach. "Maybe you should go take care of that," she laughed, pushing him to his feet.

"Oh my God," Izzy squealed, looking up from her screen. "You are not going to believe what Kelsey just posted on Instagram! Halle, you have to see this, you are going to die!"

"Positive you don't want to come with me?" Alex asked, winking.

"No, thanks. I think I'll stay here with Iz."

Alex didn't really understand why girls loved to gossip so much. Personally, half the things that came out of his sister's mouth drove him crazy.

Izzy popped up, cocked her head to the side, and stuck out her tongue, pushing Alex out of the way before taking his spot next to Halle. "Ha!"

"Okay, I get it. Be back in a few."

Halle mouthed the word *sorry* to Alex as Izzy shoved a screen in her face.

The queue for the cafeteria snaked out into the hall. Alex grimaced, his stomach protesting. Dipping his hand into the front pocket of his faded jeans, he pulled out a handful of coins, three dollars and sixty-seven cents in change.

"Sweet," he said to himself, spotting a row of vending machines. When they got back on campus they could order a pizza from the joint down the road. The thought of pepperoni covered in melting cheese made his mouth water. He fed the coins through the slot of the nearest candy machine, deciding on a couple of Kit Kat bars. Halle loved Kit Kats. He would give her a bite if he had any left.

Not wanting to head back to the girls' booth to listen to whatever Izzy had discovered while on her phone, Alex headed for the car deck. He liked checking out what people drove. No one ever stayed down on the car deck during the hour-and-forty-minute crossing from Horseshoe Bay to Nanaimo, giving him the perfect opportunity to explore and dream.

He jogged down the steps, the wind nipping at his exposed neck, and flipped up the hood of his gray sweatshirt, fumbling with the zipper until it reached the top of its track. His longer-than-usual hair whipped his eyes; he needed a haircut. The school would most likely insist he cut it to what they deemed appropriate for their male students. Alex always hated that the school dictated how they could wear their hair, but then again, there were always those individuals who liked to push the limits, so he understood their rules, for the most part. Still, he couldn't wait to get to university and start doing what he wanted for a change. Not that he would go wild but he liked his hair on the longer side, and he wanted a tattoo, something small, Greek maybe, showing off his heritage.

Alex's parents had promised to get him a car for graduation if he kept his grades up. He had applied for rowing scholarships at the University of Washington and Princeton but wouldn't hear from them regarding the status of his application for another month or so. His top choice was the UW, with their winning record and five national championships in the past six years. He'd be close to home, too, a definite perk. If he got in, it might help his chances at getting the car he wanted, too. Maybe something like that, he thought, walking up to a beautiful black vintage muscle car.

"Damn," Alex hummed, peeking inside the front passenger window of the Impala. The red vinyl seats looked in mint condition, and the dashboard still had all its original components. Even an original 8-track cassette player remained in place. "Someone loves you," he said, gently stroking the roof of the car.

Alex shivered as the wind picked up. In the distance, a car alarm sounded. He turned the corner and headed back toward the stern of the ship, hugging the inside lane next to the engine rooms where the temperature felt a little warmer. Three lanes away a car door opened. Surprised, he turned to watch.

A short man with coarse black hair, wearing a dark, striped fleece muffler, unfolded from behind the wheel of a black sedan and walked over to meet a tall, bulky man, who stood at the outside railing, next to his car, looking out. The larger guy wore a heavy Carhartt work coat and a stocking cap. Nothing but two thick metal poles and a low painted wall separated them from the icy water rushing by below. The man in the scarf spoke first, but Alex couldn't hear what he said, because the wind stole his words, pushing them into the shadows beyond the ferry.

"You left me there to rot, you son of a bitch. Five long years in a Florida prison isn't my idea of a good time!"

"What did you want me to do, Nico? If I didn't run, the cops that set up the sting would have taken our shit. Because of me we still got it."

"All of it?"

"Yeah."

"Then I want half."

"No! That wasn't the deal."

"Screw the deal. I went to jail for you. I deserve half and more."

"Like hell you do. I'm the one who got the shit through the border. I'm the one who's kept it safe."

"You ran. I had a hell of a time even finding you. I want what's mine or I'm turning you over to the DEA. You deserve to be behind bars. I bet that hot little wife of yours would even keep me company while you were locked away. What do you think? You giving me what I want or am I telling the feds how I found you?"

The taller of the two men looked out across the water while the other motioned to his chest.

"I want my money!"

A sense of unease crawled down Alex's spine. Something about the bigger man struck him as familiar, and he couldn't shake the feeling that he'd seen the giant before.

Still unable to decipher the fighting men's words, Alex ducked down behind the hood of a dark red Prius to try and get a better view of their faces. The big guy looked a lot like the school cook, Mr. Rivero, but from this angle it was hard to tell.

"You get what I say you get!" bellowed the large, familiar-looking man, slamming his fist down on the top of the other man's car while lifting him into the air with his left hand.

A strong gust combined with the roll of the ferry pushed Alex against a white BMW parked in front of the Prius, setting off the luxury car's alarm. Alex dropped to his knees as both men turned his way.

Seeing nothing, their argument escalated.

Worried that the two were going to come to blows, Alex began crawling away from them, down the narrow lane between the rows of cars, heading for the stairway leading back up to the cabin. If these guys were going to get into a fight, he should probably alert a deckhand.

Bang! Alex's ears rang, and the sound of a gunshot echoed through the deserted car deck.

Shit! Alex stopped in his tracks. His heart hammered against his rib cage. His arms and legs refused to move. Hide or run? No time! Panicking, Alex slid under the pickup truck he was next to.

From beneath the truck, Alex could see two sets of shoes. Muddied work boots were dragging suede loafers toward the low white railing. The loafers disappeared from sight, and Alex swore he heard a splash over the heavy throbbing of the ferry's diesel engines.

Burrowing his head in the crook of his elbow, Alex held his breath. The work boots paced the length of opening overlooking the water and then quickly made their way down the deck, away from the stairwell. Alex counted to fifty, then rolled from his hiding spot and sprinted up the stairs to the cabin.

CHAPTER 4

What the hell? Alex thought, stumbling into the men's washroom. He punched at the faucet of the first sink, splashing water on his face. Oil and dirt covered his arms, legs, and chest. His hands trembled under the stream of lukewarm water before he pumped out a handful of soap, scrubbing his skin until it turned red and the traces of debris were no longer visible.

Maybe it wasn't a gunshot he heard, just the guy with the loafers getting into his car, the wind slamming shut the door before he could stop it. That could be it, right? He was crawling away from the men when he heard the bang, so he didn't actually see what happened. But there were two sets of shoes when he first turned. Then the splash. There was a splash, Alex was sure of it.

Did the bigger guy push his friend over the side after he shot him? No, that couldn't be right, that crap only happens in Hollywood. This was a BC ferry, for God's sake. There were always a ton of weird noises down on the car deck.

Alex's gut twisted. He ran his wet hands through his hair. Shaking, he turned back toward the door. Should he tell the girls what he'd seen? No way, not yet; he needed to figure things out first. Like if he were going crazy. But his desire to see Halle and his sister won out, and he all but ran back to the booth where they were sitting.

Halle waved, spotting him first, and Alex felt himself breathe for the first time in minutes.

"Get something to eat?" she asked as he neared. "You don't look so good."

"Alex, where have you been? You're totally covered in dirt," Izzy said, taking in her twin brother's disheveled state.

Alex grabbed Halle's hand, pulled her to her feet, and wrapped his long arms over her shoulders, holding her close to him.

Halle could feel Alex's heartbeat through his sweatshirt. "You okay?"

Alex nodded, feeling Halle's breath on his exposed skin, willing the frantic thoughts from his mind.

Twenty minutes later, a recorded voice came over the loudspeakers. *Bing-blong.* "We are now arriving at the Nanaimo terminal. All passengers, please return to your vehicles and prepare to disembark. Foot passengers will disembark from Level Three."

CHAPTER 5

"Hey," Halle said, prodding Alex in the side with her elbow. He hadn't said a word since they boarded the bus outside the ferry terminal ten minutes earlier. The blue checked polyester seat covers scratched the bare skin on the back of her arms and she squirmed. Thinking back, he hadn't really said much at all since returning from his walk around the ferry.

"You going to tell me what's going on?" Halle raised Alex's hand to her lips and kissed the callused tips of his fingers. She felt his body shake beneath her touch.

"No," Alex replied, weaving his fingers through hers.

"Soggy fries?"

"I never got any fries. The line was too long. I didn't really eat."

Halle smiled. "Well, that explains it: low blood sugar. Your mother warned me about that."

Alex shook his head. "I grabbed a couple candy bars. It's just, I was just . . . thinking about something I saw on the car deck."

"Ha, I should have known that was where you disappeared to. See any cool cars?"

"No, it's not that. There were a couple of guys arguing, like about to get into a fist fight."

"No way."

"Yeah."

"What were they saying?"

"Couldn't really hear. They were really getting into it, though."

The back of Alex's seat started shaking.

"Yes!" Izzy squealed, shoving her face between the seats. "Tina just texted me! She's sitting in the back with Kingston, and he told her his roommate Jacob thinks I'm hot and wants to know what I'll say if he asks me to hang out. Oh my God!"

"Izzy," Halle said, pinching the bridge of her nose. "You're interrupting."

"You're always talking to Alex. Did you hear me, Halle? You know I've been crushing on Jacob all year! I'm dying!"

"What you are is annoying," Alex said. "If you like the guy so much, why don't you ask him to hang out? Jesus, Iz. Get it over with already."

"Ah . . . no? Are you nuts? I can't believe you'd even suggest such a thing! That is so not the way it's done. God, Alex."

"Iz, man, guys hate this crap. If you like him, tell him. Done."

The bus slowed to a stop, the air brakes screeching in protest.

Halle nudged Alex, raising her eyebrows.

"What?" Izzy said, looking from one to the other. "I saw that, Halle. I know you're saying something with that look, don't even try to tell me you're not."

The buses bringing students back to campus after school breaks always made two stops, one at the docks and one in the town's center. The doors eased open with a sigh. Eight more students wobbled down the aisle with bags in hand.

"Um, don't look now, Iz, but someone's getting on."

Izzy's jaw dropped as she looked toward the front.

Alex snorted a laugh. "Oh yeah, I heard he went home with Peter, since going back to Germany was out of the question. Makes sense we're picking him up here."

"Don't you dare say a word!" Izzy warned, gripping the back of Alex's seat, her knuckles turning white.

"Hey." Jacob nodded at the three sets of unblinking eyes as he approached.

Halle bit the inside of her cheek to keep herself from laughing.

Jacob's soft brown hair, neatly cut behind his ears, waved across his forehead. His elbows grazed the backs of the seats as he passed by them.

"How would you guys even kiss?" Alex whispered, making Izzy blush. "The guy's taller than I am. You'd need a stepladder."

"Don't be a jerk," Izzy hissed.

"What?" Alex shrugged. "You would. Look at him."

"Alex!" Izzy crossed her arms over her chest, hoping Jacob hadn't heard her brother.

"Izzy!"

Halle laughed. "Sorry, Iz, he does have a point."

"Whatever." Izzy eased back into her seat, clutching her phone to text her response to Tina. With a glance over her shoulder, she saw Jacob settling in two rows behind her.

"Now she's going to tell me how mean we are all night. I'll never get to bed. You know how much she likes him."

"So what, she interrupted us," Alex protested.

"She's your sister."

"I know. That's why it's so fun to tease her when she gets like this."

Halle tried to suppress her grin. "You're such a jerk."

Alex's brows rose. "Really? You want to come over here and say that to my face?"

"Yeah, maybe I do."

Alex cupped Halle's chin, pulling her lips to his.

CHAPTER 6

Lakeview Academy

Vancouver Island, British Columbia, Canada

Halle squinted against the sunlight streaming through the floor-to-ceiling windows in Mason Hall, Lakeview Academy's main dining facility. The high, buttressed ceilings of the two main wings reached thirty-five feet above the students' heads. Long, narrow tables with benches tucked beneath were grouped in rows under the different residence-house flags. Days with weather this nice were rare in early April, when rain and gloom seemed to be the norm. But not having to wear the school's dark purple raincoats over their informal uniforms felt like a treat. Even the dining hall felt lighter, warmer, more welcoming when bathed in such brilliant natural light.

Halle pushed her breakfast around her plate with the back of her fork. The eggs tasted like rubber; the bacon, sand paper. Every time she took a bite she felt like she risked choking, certain the food would get caught in her throat, sending her to the hospital. "Wow, what happened to you?" she asked, looking up to see dark circles under Alex's bright blue eyes.

Alex slid onto the bench next to Halle, below the Campbell House flag. He propped his elbows on the table, resting his head in his hands. His face looked as pale as his gray flannel trousers.

In the mornings, the students were allowed to sit at the table of their choice, unlike the other meals when they were required to sit in their house groups, girls at one table, boys at another.

"Yeah, you look like crap," Izzy said, helping herself to a rare bowl of Cocoa Krispies somebody left behind on the cereal counter. A dribble of chocolate milk dripped on her shirt, staining her white polo.

"Thanks." Alex reached for the god-awful brew the school cooks called coffee and glanced up toward the swinging doors to the kitchen just as Mr. Rivero walked through them, carrying a full tray of sausages. In his baggy white kitchen uniform, he hardly resembled the man Alex saw on the ferry yesterday, yet something still nagged at the fringe of Alex's subconscious.

Mr. Rivero unceremoniously poured the breakfast meat into the warmer on the buffet table. Bits of gristle flew from the tray, leaving shiny droplets on the floor around his feet. The pork links looked more like sticks of chalk than meat. A thick layer of grease sloshed from the side of the pan onto the table. Alex's stomach flipped as bile gathered in the back of his throat.

Halle followed her boyfriend's gaze and gagged. "Yeah, that's about enough to make me seriously consider becoming a vegetarian."

Alex lifted the heavy cream-colored mug to his lips, blowing on the molten sludge so that he could take a sip. "I couldn't sleep last night."

Giving up on her scrambled eggs, Halle put her fork down and traced her finger down Alex's back. "How come?"

Alex slouched, comfort replacing unease. "You know last night on the bus, when I told you I heard those two guys arguing down on the car deck?"

"Yeah, of course."

"Well . . . I think I heard more than them just fighting. This is going to sound crazy but I swear I heard a gun go off."

Halle's hand dropped and Izzy's spoon froze before reaching her lips.

"I didn't see anything, but the argument was getting really heated. Then this damn Beemer's alarm went off, so I ducked out of sight before the dudes could see me. I thought I should probably go get someone to break up the argument when I heard an explosion, like the ones we just heard at the gun range with your uncle."

Halle's Uncle Mike was the lead detective for the West Vancouver

Police Department. While they were visiting over the long weekend, he took them to a local gun range and taught them how to use a handgun.

"I swear it sounded just like a gun, Hal. I freaked when I heard it, like completely panicked. Dove to the ground and everything. I didn't know what else to do, so I hid under this big-ass pickup truck."

Izzy's spoon fell from her fingertips, splashing puffed brown rice and tinted milk across the table.

"Then what?" Halle said, her eyebrows arching so high they almost hit her hairline.

"At first I couldn't move, it was crazy. Then I saw their feet underneath the cars. A pair of boots, like mud-covered logger boots, then a pair of city-like loafers, kind of slick. Anyway, their shoes were standing there next to the outside railing; two pairs, then only one."

Alex didn't want to mention the splash he swore he heard, knowing it would have been next to impossible with the sound of the wind and the engines.

"And you didn't think to tell us until now?" Izzy spat.

"Well, I was about to tell Halle last night when you interrupted us on the bus." Alex sighed. "But it gets worse."

Halle blinked. "What do you mean?"

"I swear the guy who did the shooting was Mr. Rivero."

CHAPTER 7

Halle choked, pounding her fist against her chest to clear the apple juice from her lungs. "You saw the school cook shoot somebody on the ferry last night?"

Alex ground his back teeth together. "I don't know . . . I, I can't be sure, but yeah, I think I did. I've been running the scene through my head like a million times, and I keep coming to the same conclusion.

"I went down to check out the cars. You know how I like to do that. There was this sweet-looking black Impala. Totally had me drooling. Perfect condition, red interior, original gauges. Completely mint."

"Focus, Alex, for God's sake, focus," Izzy snapped. "We are talking murder here, not cars."

Alex glared at his sister.

"Did you get a good look at the men's faces?" Halle asked.

"Not really. They were looking out at the water. One guy was short, had a scarf wrapped around his neck, the other tall, like giant big." Alex nodded in Mr. Rivero's direction. "Like him." The school cook's abnormal size was often the butt of cruel student jokes. "The short guy looked cold. Kept rubbing his arms."

Halle chewed her lower lip.

"The big guy wore a stocking hat, no hair showing, looked like he might be bald. Most of the time their backs were to me. But they had dark skin; not black, but like deep Hispanic, maybe Cuban or something." Alex flicked his wrist with his thumb extended, pointing again to Mr. Rivero.

Halle wiped the remains of her juice from her lips with the back of her hand. "So, because the guy was bald and Cuban you automatically assume it had to be Mr. Rivero?"

Alex took a deep breath, holding it for several seconds. "How many big-ass, bald, Cuban-looking men do you think there are on Vancouver Island, Halle?"

"More than just one," Halle argued.

Alex shook his head. "I'm telling you, I really think the guy who did the shooting was Mr. Rivero."

"No way," Izzy said. "Halle's right. There's got to be a ton of people who look like that on this island. Not just him."

Across the room, Mr. Rivero wiped his hands on his grease-stained apron and returned to the kitchen with an empty stainless steel platter.

"He can't even cook," Izzy said. "No way could he kill someone."

Alex pushed back from the table with his palms. "This is exactly why I didn't tell you guys about this yesterday."

"Hey!" Halle gripped Alex's arm, stopping him from walking away. "I'll tell you what. I'll call Uncle Mike after classes and have him look into whether the police have heard anything about a guy getting killed last night. If things happened like you said, someone's bound to have reported the shooting by now. There would have been an abandoned car to report on the ferry, at the very least."

"You know Mike won't talk about an ongoing case, Hal."

"Yeah, that's if there is one. But I got a box full of European chocolates Mom just sent me that I'll use as a bargaining chip if he sounds reluctant. No one can say no to good chocolate."

Alex inhaled deeply before sitting back down. She was right. Until they knew more, he needed to chill. Looping his arm over Halle's shoulder, he pulled her against him. "Fine, you win for now."

CHAPTER 8

Cleaning up after the over-privileged brats at Lakeview Academy was not what Lola had in mind when they fled Florida. She missed her friends, family, the days of endless sun. Sure, Ramon got them a house when they arrived in Canada—the house was much better than the beat-up trailer they had in Miami—but he never said shit about how cold the place got or mentioned anything about all the goddamn rain. Their roof grew moss. What the hell? The people who liked it here were freakin' crazy. Lola thought they were all smoking crack. Sure, the sun was out today. She'd been here two years now and could count on one hand how many times the weather had been warm enough to wear her favorite bikini, the light blue one with the fringe that made the men around her stare like they did when she was seventeen.

There was sun and there was heat; Canada had nothing on Florida when it came to heat. She longed to go back. She wanted to wear her short shorts and tube tops and strut around in her collection of stilettos, now piled in a box at the back of her closet, collecting dust. If she tried to wear her six-inch spiked heels here she'd sink in the mud. The people around here wore flannel and fleece most of the year. The thought of something so ugly against her skin made her cringe.

Lola cursed as she broke another nail. The cleaners the school used made them weak, impossible to maintain.

She snapped her gum, then blew a tight bubble through her teeth. These people ain't never seen what real good weather looks like, she thought.

Crummy weather and then there was their new last name: Rivero. How lame. However, she was glad Ramon let them keep their first names. They were common enough, he said. Hundreds of Cuban Americans shared them. But the last name . . . She liked Ramon's real last name, Perez, much better. Changing their name to fit their new identities hadn't been optional, though, nor was moving to Canada, as its border was the easiest to cross once their new identity papers came through.

Posing as cooks, however, that had been her idea. Years of working in restaurants, trying to bring in a little more cash so they could move out of the trailer park, taught her how to manage a kitchen. It also taught her how to pose as someone in the industry. Thanks to a couple with the last name Rivero, who came in looking for a job, it also provided her with social security numbers. Those Riveros had been big shots, nutritionists; too good for the place she used to work at. They ended up heading over to Europe, opening a place of their own in Spain or some such place, giving Lola the perfect identities to steal. Now, she had credit cards and everything in her new name. As long as she always paid everything off and kept on the right side of the law, no one would ever know better.

Only four tables remained to be cleaned. "Stupid kids," she said under her breath, looking at their occupants. That was another thing that got to her. Working at a school. But Ramon insisted, saying the money was good, and it would be easy to go unnoticed. He worked the background checks with a buddy of his, a computer hacker he met in jail when he served a six-month sentence for petty theft. Paid extra, even, to get their fake visas.

Lola looked down at her ruined manicure, the fuchsia polish chipped beyond repair. What she wouldn't give for a decent place to have her nails done, a proper acrylic set, at least an inch in length. Screw that; what she wouldn't give to have a job that didn't require a hair net. Lola scratched at the polyester uniform they forced her to wear. The hideous fabric did nothing for her figure.

The Shakira song on her iPod ended. "Damn," she swore, taking the device from her pocket. Two tables over from her, three kids huddled in conversation. One of the girls turned toward her, the taller one, sitting next to the boy. She watched Lola fiddle with her music player for a second before turning back to her friends.

"I'm telling you both, the guy who pulled the trigger was Mr. Rivero," the boy was saying.

Lola's eye twitched. Of all the stupid-ass things her oaf of a husband had done since they left Florida, Lola still couldn't believe Ramon murdered their old partner Nico. Yeah, yeah, the guy deserved to be offed, wanting a bigger cut of their money like that, but, damn, Ramon shouldn't have killed him in public! And now they have a witness? Great! She knew someone would've seen, although of course he swore no one did. And a goddamn student, too. Unbelievable!

Lola moved to the table next to the kids. She put her earbuds back in, pretending to dance to the nonexistent beat so they wouldn't think she was listening.

"No way," said the girl sitting across from the boy. She then made a smart-ass remark about Ramon's cooking.

Ungrateful brat. Lola closed her eyes and prayed for patience, hoping Nico's wouldn't be the only murder resting on their shoulders.

The girls didn't believe the boy. Thank God for that, Lola thought.

A glass shattered across the room, yanking her attention away from the kids' table.

"*Mierda*," she cursed, shoving her stained bleach rag into the pocket of her apron.

CHAPTER 9

The hair on the back of Halle's arms stood on end. Why was the kitchen lady looking at them like she wanted to hurt them? The woman creeped her out. When Halle glanced behind her a second time, to make sure she wasn't seeing things, the woman had apparently lost interest, a mess made by some other students taking her to the other side of the hall.

"Thank God," Halle said, shaking off the uneasy feeling left by the kitchen aide's malicious glare.

Alex looked at her. "Did you say something?"

"No," Halle replied, reminding herself that her brain tended to exaggerate things on occasion.

Alex kissed the side of her neck. "I love you," he whispered, his warm breath teasing the base of her ear. Halle leaned into his lips.

"Ew, okay, seriously, you two, cut it with the PDA at the breakfast table. You're grossing me out," Izzy said.

"Jealous much?" Alex teased.

"Hey, guys," Jacob said, walking up to the table. His caramel-colored hair shot out in four different directions, like he had forgotten to use a comb or else just rolled out of bed. Even his gray uniform trousers and red polo had that "just woke up" look.

"Hey, Jacob," Halle said, since Izzy had suddenly grown speechless.

Jacob's dark eyes locked on Izzy, and his hopeful smile reminded Halle of a golden retriever puppy.

"Halle texted me. She said you wanted to talk, Izzy."

Izzy looked like a deer caught in the headlights.

"Yeah, remember, Iz?" Halle coached. "About French? Jacob's fluent. I told him you were having troubles keeping up with the class and he offered to help you out."

Jacob smiled, his white teeth dazzling in the morning sun.

Izzy pulled herself together, squaring her shoulders, her cheeks turning the same color as Jacob's shirt. "Yeah, yeah . . . that's right," she stammered. "French."

"Hey, man," Alex said. "Have a seat."

Jacob scooted onto the bench next to Izzy.

"Thanks for coming over," Izzy managed to get out.

Under the table, Halle felt one of her best friend's black school flats connect with her shin. Wincing, she added, "Yeah, Izzy needs all the help she can get."

•

Lola watched the kids' table through the circular window in the swinging kitchen door, her blood pressure rising. After a couple minutes, the boy who'd mentioned her husband stood up with the others, grabbed his book bag from a hook near the main door, an old leather thing like what the postmen in old movies carried, and left for classes. She needed to do something about him. Shut him up before he could put things together. If their cover was blown and the kid somehow linked Ramon to Nico's murder, they would lose everything. She worked too hard covering their tracks to get busted now, and Ramon finally found a buyer for the coke, all of it, which meant in a couple of weeks this whole charade would be over. They could pack up, maybe move somewhere warm again. Five long years they'd waited to make this deal. She'd be damned if some stupid kid would stand in their way now.

"Ramon! Get your ass over here!" Lola yelled.

"What?"

"We got a problem."

"Yeah?"

Lola turned, meeting his narrow, black gaze. "But I think I got an idea about how to deal with it."

CHAPTER 10

Halle stood on the steps, one riser above Alex, looking him in the eyes, just inside the main door of the English building.

"You're frowning," she said. "Still thinking about Mr. Rivero?"

Alex nodded reluctantly. "How can you tell?"

Halle traced the deepest line with the tip of her finger. "I thought we agreed you'd stop worrying about it until I could talk to my uncle."

"I can't stop. The images won't leave my head."

"The sound could've been a car door or something else slamming. There are tons of things that go on down there. Remember what your mom is always telling us? Ninety percent of the things we worry about never end up happening. You'll see."

"I know, but the whole thing's really messing with my head."

Halle wrapped her arms around Alex's neck, pulling his unshaven face against the side of her cheek. "Someone forgot to shave."

Alex smiled, his hands gripping Halle's waist just above the top of her kilt.

Twice a week and to chapel services, the students had to wear their formal uniforms with blazers and ties. The rest of the time they were allowed to wear a less formal version, consisting of kilts or trousers, polos, and a nice V-neck jumper with the school crest on it.

Alex kissed Halle's jaw, dragging his stubble across her face.

"Stop it," Halle giggled. "You know that tickles."

"I can't. I like making you laugh."

Wyatt Donley, Alex's roommate, exited the room where Alex and Halle shared their third period. His pale face and white-blond hair made him look ghostlike. If not for the disparaging smile spread over his thin lips, Halle would have thought him more undead zombie than human. His angular face hardened. "You know, there's a motel down the road."

Halle extended her middle finger. "Bite me."

Wyatt threw his head back, laughing. His hair barely moved under a thick coating of gel. "Oh, so now it's me you want. My roommate not enough man for you?"

"I wouldn't touch you if you were the last man on earth, Wyatt."

Alex rolled his eyes. "Dude, what are you doing?"

Wyatt shook his head. "Nothing, man, just having a little fun with your girl."

"Not in the mood." Alex exhaled, shaking his head.

Wyatt tossed his book bag over his shoulder. "Whatever."

Halle watched Wyatt disappear from sight. "God, he's an arrogant jerk. I can't believe you have to live with him."

"He's only trying to get under your skin, Hal. If you ignore him, he'll go away."

"That's not the point. You shouldn't have to cohabitate with a guy like that."

Halle pushed against Alex's chest, trying to break from the circle of his arms.

"Oh no you don't," Alex warned, pulling her back. "Besides, he's not that bad one on one, and he doesn't have many friends. He needs me."

"He needs something, that's for sure."

"Come on. He can't help that he's an idiot, Hal. It's like a survival mechanism for him. He's from Toronto, for God's sake. It wasn't his choice to go to Lakeview. His mum forced him to go here because she didn't want him messing up her life at home. If you knew half the crap he puts up with you'd feel sorry for him too. Who knows, if you two tried to stop hating each other so much, you'd probably end up getting along."

"He's the one who started it."

"Yeah, but you don't help by going off on him every time he says something."

Halle looked away.

"I only react because he's mean, Alex. He verbally abuses me every time he sees us together. I'm not going to sit there and not say anything. I have to defend myself."

Alex took a deep breath. "I know, I know. You're right. But in a fair fight you could probably take him. I think you're taller. You're definitely feistier."

Halle sighed, chewing her lower lip.

"Did I tell you that when he first saw you last fall, he actually told me you were hot? I almost had to beat the crap out of him."

"Why didn't you?"

Alex laughed, the sound coming from deep in his belly. "'Cause getting booted out of school didn't seem worth it to me. Besides, as soon as he saw me with you he backed off. It's probably why he goes out of his way to pick on you. He's just embarrassed he said something in the first place."

"Right, that makes sense. Alex, Wyatt's just an arrogant pig that thinks the whole world should revolve around him. I doubt he's ever been embarrassed about anything."

"You'd be surprised. The most insecure guys often put up the biggest show."

"Dr. Phil-ing on me now, big guy?" Halle said, giving up on Alex ever understanding her dislike for his roommate.

Alex smiled. Reaching down, he picked up both of their book bags in one hand. "Come on, smartass, let's go," he said, motioning to the now open classroom door. "Unless, of course, you want me to analyze something else for you?"

With a shake of her head, Halle followed. "Not a chance."

CHAPTER 11

"Hey, wait up!" Izzy yelled after classes, taking the steps two at a time that led up to Campbell House, the dorm she and Halle called home for the last four years.

"So you're talking to me again?" Halle teased.

"Of course I'm talking to you. Just don't embarrass me like that again . . . bitch." A slow smile spread across Izzy's face, reassuring Halle that she was no longer in trouble. "Plus I have gossip."

Halle's eyebrow rose. "Do tell."

"Guess who has a study date tonight?"

"So my French-tutor scheme worked?"

Izzy blushed. "Maybe."

"Where are you guys going?"

"He's ordering pizza, and we're meeting in the common room of his dorm."

"Where does he live again?"

"Drake."

"Oh yeah, that's right. I remember his red house shirt this morning." Halle started up the second set of steps. "You know, my shin is bruised now because of you."

The bright blue eyes Izzy shared with her brother twinkled. "Wimp!"

Halle changed shoulders with her backpack as Izzy tried to match her pace. In grade 8, they had been roughly the same size; now, not so much. Halle could easily see over Izzy's head when they were standing toe to toe.

"Why are you in such a rush to get back to the House?"

"I told Alex I'd call Uncle Mike at the office, and I don't want to miss him."

"So, do you really think he saw Mr. Rivero?"

"No, but I promised him I would call. A promise is a promise. Besides, it will make your brother feel better if he knows that the police are looking into it as well."

Out of the corner of her eye, Halle noticed Wyatt tossing a rugby ball on the small patch of grass between his house, Lockhart, and hers. Both Tudor-style dormitories sat on the hill to the right of Lakeview's main campus, above the headmaster's own house. To the left, freshly mowed lawns rolled down to the lake while a tree-lined drive wound through the campus to the school's academic buildings below.

Wyatt's perfectly coifed hair looked exactly like it had earlier in the day, not a piece out of place. Shaking her head, Halle wondered how much he spent on his appearance. His sweats even bore designer labels. Why couldn't he just wear the school stuff like the rest of the student body? "I hate him," she mumbled.

"I know!" said Izzy, following her roommate's gaze, instantly knowing to whom she referred.

Wyatt caught the ball then swaggered back up to his mates before kicking it to the group gathered on the far side of the open lawn, waiting to receive the punt.

"I don't get what people see in him." Izzy sighed.

Halle shook her head. "Me neither."

"Oh my God, did you hear? He and Missy totally got together last night."

Halle gagged. "What? Okay, I think I just barfed in my mouth."

"Gross," Izzy said, swatting Halle with the back of her hand.

"Seriously, I am going to be sick. Tell me you just made that up!"

"Afraid not. She's been bragging about hooking up with him all day. Even in chem. class, and we were taking a test!"

"Do you think either of them ever talk about anyone but themselves? How do you fit that much ego around one table? What do they even do besides look in the mirror and compliment themselves when they get together?"

"Well, according to Missy, Wyatt brought a huge bag of pot back to campus after break, and the two of them are going up to the old quarry this weekend and getting 'totally wasted,'" Izzy said, finger-quoting.

Halle stopped just outside the front doors to Campbell House. "You're kidding, right? She can't seriously be telling people that? And Alex said Wyatt didn't smoke anymore. What a laugh. Why am not surprised?"

Izzy held the heavy glass-paneled door to their dorm open.

Halle closed her eyes, kneading her forehead with the palm of her hand. "Jesus, could Missy be stupider? Does she even get how dangerous it is to talk about that kind of crap on campus?"

"Excuse me?" the person in question said, gliding down the main staircase leading to the girls' rooms on the top two floors. "Are you talking about me?"

Halle took a deep breath. Missy's fake platinum-blond hair showed a good inch of grow-out. "Why, Missy, what perfect timing."

Missy trailed a well-manicured crimson nail down the stair rail, tapping her index finger several times against the wooden bar before releasing it at the last step. Her matching, heavily painted lips pursed.

"Oh, is that a new color of polish?" Izzy asked, quickly stepping forward.

Missy waved her fingers in the air. "Totally. Mummy and I just had them done last weekend. They're gel."

"Wow, they look great. I'll have to try that soon," Izzy said, sounding friendly.

"Iz, are you coming or not?" Halle snarled, stomping up the stairs.

"Be right there."

Halle slammed open the fire door separating the bedrooms from the stairwell.

Getting caught with drugs or even talking about having drugs on campus was about *the* stupidest thing a student could do at Lakeview Academy. First offence—instant suspension; second offence—automatic expulsion. If a teacher even caught wind of something going on, the student-in-question's room would be thoroughly searched and their roommates could be questioned. The thought of Alex possibly having to go through the stress of something like that after everything else going on because of Missy's big mouth made Halle want to punch something.

"You know, it wouldn't kill you to try and be nice occasionally," Izzy said, catching up to Halle.

"To her? You can't be serious. I haven't bothered being nice to her since she accused me of cutting her hair while she was asleep, back in grade 8. Why the hell would I start now?"

"I'm just saying it wouldn't hurt. Especially if she's hanging out with your boyfriend's roommate."

CHAPTER 12

Halle threw herself on her bed, her brown and blue Pottery Barn duvet wrapping her in downy bliss. The matching monogrammed pillow her mom insisted she get bounced to the floor. "Sorry, Iz. It's just, you know how crazy Missy makes me."

"Yeah, I know. But you have to learn to let it go sometimes."

Halle shook her head. "You know, you're the second person today to tell me that, your brother being the first."

Izzy smiled. "Well, maybe you should start listening to us."

Halle stuck her tongue out and reached for her phone.

"West Vancouver Police Department, how may I help you?"

"Hi, Sheri, it's Halle. Is Uncle Mike there?"

"Sure, sweetheart, just a second." Canned music hummed through the earpiece.

"Hey, Kiddo."

Halle grinned as her mother's brother's deep voice finally filled in where some unidentified '80s tune left off. "Hi, Uncle Mike."

"How was your ride back to school?"

"Okay. Thanks again for having us. It was an awesome weekend."

"Any time. You know your Auntie Arlene and I love having you guys stay with us. I just wish you weren't graduating this year and moving back to Europe."

Halle didn't really want to leave the area behind her forever either. She loved western Canada's rugged appeal. "I'll be back after university, Uncle Mike. You can't take the Northwest away from a girl like me for too long."

"So, to what do I owe the pleasure of your call?"

Halle swallowed, feeling nervous at having to ask her uncle such an obtuse question. "Well, I . . . I have a favor to ask."

"Shoot."

"Do you know if anyone got shot or went missing last night on the West Van-to-Nanaimo ferry run we were on?"

Halle heard the front legs of her uncle's tipped chair hit the floor.

"Excuse me?"

Halle cringed as she imagined his square jaw tightening. "Don't ask."

Uncle Mike's voice turned firm. "You can't exactly drop a bomb of a question like that Halle and expect me not to inquire why you're asking."

Halle inhaled slowly before answering then repeated the whole of Alex's story.

"Hmm," Uncle Mike said, his voice strained. "I'm not sure how to reply. I can check with the recent missing persons reports to police in the area, see if there was an abandoned car on one of the ferry runs, and make a couple calls, but besides that I'm not sure what else I can do."

"Thanks, Uncle Mike. That would be great."

"Kiddo?"

"Yeah?"

"Do me a favor."

"Sure."

"If this does turn out to be something, don't get involved in it this time. You and your sister have a nasty habit of turning my hair gray."

The knot in Halle's chest released, and she laughed. "You worry too much, Uncle Mike. Besides, *I* didn't see anything. Just Alex. You're the best. Give Auntie Arlene a kiss for me."

"Will do."

"Love you."

"Love you too."

Halle grinned as she set her phone down.

"How'd it go?" Izzy asked.

"Good. He said he'd check into it. I didn't even have to bribe him with Mom's chocolates."

"Awesome! Does that mean we can eat them now?"

Halle got up and grabbed the box hidden under a textbook resting on her top shelf. "Dig in."

CHAPTER 13

Tuesday afternoons were Halle's least favorite sporting practices. Her mom called her lazy, but in truth, Halle just didn't like being forced to work out in a gym on a dry day. Too many sweaty bodies, never enough ventilation.

"Seriously, just because I can do ten good pull-ups in a row doesn't mean I should have to do three more sets of twelve," Halle complained from her treadmill. "Do you have some hand sanitizer by the way? That pull-up bar is disgusting." Halle toweled the sweat from her face.

"I know!" Trisha, a girl from Halle's four-person rowing shell running on the treadmill next to hers, agreed.

Rows of treadmills and ergometers were lined up parallel to each other on black foam mats, stationary bicycles and weight machines behind them. The white painted walls reflected the alien glow of florescent lights, giving Halle a headache.

Smack! Alex's hand collided with Halle's upper leg, leaving five distinct finger impressions. "Five star!"

"Ow!"

"Got ya!"

The guys' senior eight boat played a warped slapping game called five star, thinking it was cool to leave their full handprints on girls' thighs.

The smug grin on her boyfriend's face made Halle laugh. She took in his shirtless torso. Baggy black shorts hung from his narrow hips, showing off his perfect abs. "I'll get you back for that."

"I know." Alex beamed.

"Just remember, revenge is a dish best served cold," Halle said.

"I'm looking forward to it."

Halle slowed her machine to a stop. "Come with me," she said, jumping off and grabbing Alex's arm.

"What, can't wait to meet up later? Got to have a little of me now?"

Halle shook her head. "Seriously? Full of yourself much today?"

Alex grinned back, his eyes teasing.

The last traces of daylight glowed orange on the horizon as Halle pulled him through the main gym doors. They stood alone on the asphalt path to the left of the building.

"Okay, I like the way you think," Alex said, pulling Halle against his sweat-drenched chest.

"Alex!" Halle exclaimed, frustrated that he wasn't taking her seriously when he tried to kiss her. "I did not bring you out here to make out."

"Sucks for you." He covered her lips with his.

Halle pushed hard against her boyfriend's chest. "Stop."

Still holding Halle in his arms, Alex froze.

"Listen, I talked to my uncle."

Halle felt him take a deep breath, his rib cage rising against hers. "And?"

"He said he hadn't heard anything, but he would call around, maybe check the missing persons reports."

Alex bowed his head. "So we wait?"

Halle nodded. "Yup."

"Okay."

"Alex, if something did happen on that ferry, Uncle Mike will call. Don't worry."

"Easier said than done."

Halle reached behind his back, running her fingers down his spine.

"Dumas, Henry, get back in here!" Alex's coach yelled, throwing the door to the weight room open, the use of their last names indicating he would make them run if they didn't hurry.

"Crap," Halle groaned.

Alex forced a smile to his face. "Come on, lazy butt. Let's get this practice over with."

CHAPTER 14

Halle blinked, her pulsating phone waking her from the AP Calculus-homework coma. Yawning, she checked the screen. The text made her smile.

•

April 7, 2015 8:30 PM
Alex: Come down and play.

•

Halle ran to the window. Alex stood below, grinning broadly, a blanket tucked under his arm. Cold air rushed in as she cranked open the pane.

"What are you doing?"

"Mr. Scott told me you could see both of Saturn's moons from the new telescope in the observatory. Let's go check it out."

Halle looked to the sky. Stars sparkled overhead like diamonds against black velvet. Clear nights on campus always amazed her, the skies so much darker than at home because there were no city lights interfering with their visibility.

She nodded. "Be right there." Halle grabbed her thick purple school fleece, throwing it over her Kygo concert T-shirt, and tucked her yoga pants into the sheepskin lining of her new favorite UGG boots.

"Where are you going?" Izzy asked, coming out of the bathroom, her hair brushed, fresh color staining her lips.

"I think the question should be where are you going?" Halle said, noticing her roommate's refreshed appearance. "You look good."

Izzy flushed pink. "What do you mean?"

"Um, that outfit is to die for. Seriously, love the skinny jeans with that sweater."

"Thanks. Jacob's coming over to get me. We're going to watch a movie in his house's common room."

"So I'm guessing your study date went well?"

"Maybe . . ."

Halle shook her head, laughing. "Just remember, take things slowly with him." Izzy had a nasty habit of falling for guys quickly, doing things she regretted, then getting dumped.

"I will. Jacob's different, anyway. He's nice. Like really nice."

"Yeah, heard that one before." Halle ducked as Izzy threw a pillow at her head. "Hey!" she squealed. "Don't say I didn't warn you."

Izzy heard Alex's voice coming from outside their window.

"Hal-lee . . ."

Halle grinned. "Gotta go!"

A minute later, Izzy watched from their window as her roommate flew into her brother's arms.

"Come on." Alex grabbed Halle's hand, pulling her away from the dorm, his fingers weaving through hers, warming her entire body with his touch.

Halle brought his knuckles to her lips, kissing each one in order starting with his pinky.

"Watch out, little girl, or I'll let you kiss a lot more than just my hand."

Halle giggled. "Oh yeah?"

The light from the full moon lit the path in front of them.

"Hey," Jacob said to Alex and Halle as he passed them heading into Campbell House.

"Hey, man," Alex returned.

"Have fun," Halle called over her shoulder as Alex led her toward the school's new solarium near the upper soccer fields.

"But not too much," Alex warned.

Halle playfully swatted Alex's chest with her free hand. "What was that about?"

"She *is* my sister."

"Duh."

"So it's not exactly like I want to think of her doing this." Alex pulled Halle into his chest, sealing her mouth with his lips. Coming up for air, he stepped back, gently pushing her away.

"I see," Halle sighed.

"Good, now come on. I don't want to miss this."

Dazed, Halle chewed on her lower lip, swollen from Alex's kiss. "Whatever you say, Galileo."

CHAPTER 15

Halle entered the dining hall for lunch the next day and stood at the balcony overlooking the tables, scanning the crowded room. "Do you know where your brother is?" she asked Izzy, who walked in behind her. "Alex never showed up for breakfast or his first class. I tried texting but he still hasn't responded."

"Why would I know where he is? He's your boyfriend. You talk to him more than I do." Izzy dumped her backpack on the floor, covering it with her coat.

Halle scowled. "I haven't heard from him all morning. I just thought maybe you had."

A hand grabbed her wrist, startling her.

"Hey."

Halle's worried expression eased. "Where have you been?"

"Why? Worried about me?"

"Duh, yeah."

Alex looked pleased at Halle's admission. "Sorry, my alarm never went off this morning."

"It's okay. Did you finally get some sleep?" Halle placed her hand on Alex's cheek, looking at the dark circles still shadowing his eyes.

"No, not really, that's why I didn't hear my alarm. I think I finally dozed off around five."

"Ouch, that sucks."

"Tell me about it. Mr. Lane freaked when I wasn't in class. He already contacted my advisor. Now I have to go to tutorials in his office after classes to get help with the work I missed."

"Yeah, he didn't seem too happy about you not being there. He kept asking me where you were, and since I didn't know, I started to get a little freaked out."

"Aw, that's kind of cute. I did text you, though."

Halle reached into her blouse and pulled her cell phone from her bra.

"Do you have to keep your phone in there?" Alex groaned, watching her.

"Yeah, everyone else does. Besides, these stupid skirts don't have pockets, and it's not raining so I can't stash the thing in my boots. Anyway, Kelsey's phone was taken from her pack last week, and if I lose or break another phone, my mom will kill me. No way I want the 'you need to be more responsible' lecture."

Halle punched in her lock code and opened her messages.

Looking over her shoulder, Alex saw his name appear several times on the screen. "See, told you I tried to get a hold of you."

"Whatever. They must have just come in."

Alex shrugged, having no clue why she didn't get them immediately.

Benches screeched as students maneuvered into places around the tables.

"Meet you after lunch? I'll walk you to your next class to make up for earlier," Alex said.

"Are you going to carry my books for me, too?" Halle taunted.

Alex grinned. "Only if you let me put that phone back for you."

Halle playfully pushed Alex's shoulder, blushing. "Yeah, right, like that's going to happen."

After putting her phone securely back in place, Halle wove through the long tables to the one set up beneath the Campbell house flag. So Harry Potter, she thought, happier now that she knew Alex was okay.

"*Salut*," Izzy said in French, plopping down next to her roommate at their assigned table.

"Hmm, sounds like your foreign language studies are progressing nicely, now that you have a tutor."

Izzy nudged Halle's shoulder with her own. "*Merci beaucoup*. I believe they are."

Halle laughed. "Now how do you say 'pass the grilled cheese sandwiches' in French?"

The girl next to Izzy set the sandwich platter down in front of her. "Please tell me they did not use the French toast they served for breakfast last week to make these sandwiches!" Processed cheese slices oozed oil from between two browned, egg-battered slices of bread.

Halle leaned forward, looking around Izzy to see for herself. "Oh God, I think it is."

"Girls?" Their housemother, Mrs. Middleton, stood behind them, placing a hand on each of their shoulders. "Is something the matter?"

"No, Mrs. Middleton." Izzy winced and passed the tray to a housemate across the table. "Halle and I were just discussing the possibility of eating from the salad bar this afternoon."

Mrs. Middleton didn't look convinced. "Is that so?"

Halle nodded. "Yup, I'm totally craving carrots."

Izzy agreed. "Definitely."

CHAPTER 16

Lola watched the students file into Mason Hall from the conference room in the upper right-hand mezzanine. Pushing back her rough cuticles with the edge of her paint-chipped thumbnail, she took note of where the kids placed their packs.

"There," she murmured, seeing the student and bag she sought. At six foot four, the boy was easy to spot. She watched as he hung his things on one of the pegs in the upper gallery where the students were required to leave their belongings while they ate at the tables below.

His name was Alex, if she remembered right. Over the three years they'd been at the school she had watched him grow from a scrawny string bean into a handsome young man. She almost felt guilty about what she had to do next. Damn Ramon for leaving so many loose ends. She fingered the roughly taped tan wax paper bag in her apron pocket. Inside it was a Ziploc bag with less than a half-ounce of marijuana. Not a lot, but enough to get the boy kicked out.

She would tell a couple of her friends who liked to hang out in the teacher's lounge that she'd seen this Alex kid stick something funny in his bag and that he smelled a lot like skunk weed when he passed her in the dining hall. If she raised her voice just a little when she spoke, the whole room would hear. The school was on crackdown-mode these days with its new zero-tolerance drug policy. If the right faculty members overheard her talking about her "suspicions," the news would make it to the main office by the end of the day and the boy would be searched. No one would even be able to track the drugs back to her, unless they wanted to admit they'd been eavesdropping, which she knew they wouldn't. Now, all she had to do was plant the evidence.

Lola ran her hands down the front of her apron, adjusting the stained fabric to cover the rip in her stockings.

Unnoticed, she moved toward the grouping of carefully hung backpacks, trying not to trip over the bulk of the bags littering the floor. Stopping in front of her target, Lola took a deep breath and reached for the leather satchel. Quickly, she pushed the drugs deep into one of the two outer pockets.

That should do it, she thought confidently, patting the worn exterior, making sure her package was secure.

CHAPTER 17

"Class be seated," said Mr. Klein, the AP language teacher, pushing his wire-framed glasses farther up his nose.

Alex reached into his bag and took out his copy of *The Great Gatsby*.

Halle, next to him, put her spiral notebook on the table. "Need a pen?" she asked, twirling a dark blue ballpoint between her fingers.

"Yeah, as a matter of fact, I do," Alex said, leaning toward Halle's desk.

Halle's cheeks dimpled as Alex slipped the pen from her hand, holding her fingers a little longer than necessary.

Mr. Klein cleared his throat. "Open your books to twenty-three—"

The phone on the teacher's desk rang. "Hold that thought," Mr. Klein said, raising his hand, clearly annoyed by the interruption.

Halle wiggled in her seat, pulling her kilt down to cover her thighs. The cold plastic chairs were sticking to her bare legs.

"Want to run down to the village before sport?" Alex asked.

Halle smiled. "Candy craving?"

Leaning back in his chair, Alex leafed through the pages of his notebook. "Pretty much. That and I wouldn't mind getting off campus with you for a bit." He dragged his long fingers through the mop of brown curls spilling onto his forehead.

"Yeah, I think I could manage the walk."

"Mr. Dumas," Mr. Klein said, clearing his throat.

"Yes, sir." Alex was startled by the teacher's use of his name.

Halle's easy demeanor turned curious.

"Mr. Davies wants to see you in his office. Please gather your things and make your way there immediately."

A pained look swept across Alex's face. Being called into the deputy dean's office in the middle of class couldn't be good a thing. "Me?"

"Yes, Mr. Dumas. That's what I was told."

Alex swore under his breath. Mr. Davies, the deputy dean, also served as the school's head of discipline. Alex searched his memory of the last few days, sure that he hadn't done anything that would merit a visit to the man's office.

Halle reached for Alex's hand when he stood, squeezing his fingers. "It's okay. I'm sure it's nothing," she whispered as he reached for his bag.

Alex swallowed hard, his Adam's apple bobbing.

Text me, Halle mouthed as he glanced at her one last time at the door before leaving.

When Mr. Klein turned his back, Halle grabbed her phone from the front of her shirt and set it in her lap so that she could secretly text Alex back when he told her what was going on.

"So, as I was saying before we were interrupted," Mr. Klein began.

CHAPTER 18

Alex walked down the empty hallway heading toward the deputy dean's office. Since Mr. Davies was put in charge of discipline two years ago, the student expulsion rate had doubled due to his unyieldingly strict policies.

The heels of Alex's black loafers clicked against the freshly buffed wood floors, the sound echoing off the paneled walls. He adjusted the collar of his shirt, loosening it so he could breathe easier. If he was in trouble, his parents would kill him. Being from a Greek family had its perks, but it also meant stricter than average parents. The wrath of Zeus couldn't compare to his dad's temper if Alex were to get in trouble at school. Alex took a deep breath. At the end of the hall he heard Mrs. Sloan, Mr. Davies's assistant, answer the phone.

Coming through the door, Alex noticed Mrs. Sloan cover the phone's receiver with the palm of her hand. Her straight brown hair pulled into a neat bun made her narrow face look hard. Alex wondered if she liked her job. She didn't look like the kind of woman who smiled much.

"Have a seat," she said through tight lips. "I'll let Mr. Davies know you're here."

Alex fiddled with the strap of his book bag. The thick leather, worn from years of use, felt like butter between his fingertips. The bag belonged to his grandfather when he was a boy. Last summer, when he and Izzy went to Greece to visit relatives, Alex found it in his grandparents' attic. Upon asking, Ya-ya, his grandmother, offered to let him keep the old thing in exchange for his help cleaning out the unused room.

The door to the inner office swung open. "Mr. Dumas," Mr. Davies said, straightening his tie as he walked toward Alex. Mr. Davies's thick black hair, heavily streaked with gray, looked disheveled, but his tan pleated trousers, blue wool blazer, and perfectly ironed, pristine white shirt were immaculate. "Follow me."

Alex's heart gave a thud. "Sorry, sir, but I'm not really sure why I'm here. Can you please tell me why I've been called in to your office?"

Mr. Davies scowled then motioned to the ridged, high-backed chair next to his desk. "Place your book bag on the desk and then take a seat, Mr. Dumas."

Mr. Davies opened the drawer on the right side of his desk and pulled out a plastic cup with a light blue screw cap. "I need a urine sample," he said simply, pushing the container toward Alex.

Alex's jaw dropped. "Excuse me?"

"You are taking a mandatory drug test."

"The hell I am."

"I would watch my tongue if I were you, Mr. Dumas. You have been an exemplary student up to this point, but swearing will not improve your situation." Mr. Davies's unrelenting steel-gray eyes held Alex's stare, demanding he obey. "Take the container," he ordered.

"But I don't understand."

"I think you do."

Alex couldn't fathom why Mr. Davies insisted on treating him like a hardened criminal. Except for one time in grade 9, before Mr. Davies occupied the deputy's office, he'd never been in trouble with the school. "No. Why do you think I'm doing drugs?"

"This is not a part of my job that I enjoy. We have alerted your housefather. He is searching your room as we speak." Mr. Davies's eyes lowered to the drug test sitting on his tidy desk. "I would suggest you do as I have asked."

"Can you at least tell me what it is you think I'm doing?"

"Mr. Dumas, I have been made aware of the fact that you may be using and in possession of cannabis."

"No way!"

Mr. Davies cocked his head.

Angry now, Alex grabbed the cup. "You're wrong."

"I hope so. When you are finished, please leave the test on the bathroom counter."

"Have a seat, Mr. Dumas," Mr. Davies instructed when Alex returned.

Mrs. Sloan knocked on the door. "The test came back negative," she said.

"Thank you."

Alex inhaled. "So can I go now?"

"No, there is one more thing we have to do. Open your bag, please."

"Are you serious?"

"Yes, Mr. Dumas."

Alex unhooked the heavy metal buckles on either side of his bag's leather flap.

"Now, empty it."

Alex did as he was told, his hands shaking in anger.

"As you know, Mr. Dumas, the school does not take drug use lightly."

Alex placed two spiral notebooks, a three-ring binder, two pencils, a Sharpie, and the blue ballpoint pen Halle just loaned him on the desk.

"The outside bit as well," Mr. Davies said, pointing.

Alex rolled his eyes. "I don't even use those pockets."

"Check them, please."

Opening the first one, Alex's fingers hit paper, slick to the touch. "What the—?"

Mr. Davies cocked his head. "Well?"

Alex held in his hand the waxed bag Lola had hidden. He looked up at the deputy dean, his expression a mix of confusion and fear. "This isn't mine."

Mr. Davies's eyes narrowed. "Unfortunately, I've heard that before.

Please pass it to me."

"But seriously, sir, whatever that is, it's not mine. I've never seen it before."

Mr. Davies grimaced. Sliding one of his bony fingers beneath the folded, taped edge, he opened it. "This is your second offence, is it not?"

Alex's face blanched. In Mr. Davies's hand sat a small plastic bag with two large, dried green buds.

"No, I mean yes, sir, but I never smoked or drank anything in grade 9. The records should show that. I was put on probation and given work hours for being present but never punished for actual consumption. The school let me go with the minimum because I'd only just walked into the room when the teacher arrived."

"I've read the file, Mr. Dumas. Regardless of what happened, the fact remains that this is not the first time you've been in trouble."

"Sir?"

Mr. Davies shook his head. "I believe the evidence speaks for itself."

"But my piss test was clean! I'm not doing drugs!"

"Yes, but they were found in your possession. School regulations clearly state that a second drug-related offence results in automatic expulsion.

Mr. Davies's phone rang. "Yes, Mrs. Sloan?

"Mr. Dumas, please have a seat in the hall."

CHAPTER 19

Where the hell was Alex? His seat had remained empty for the entire fifty-five-minute block, making Halle wonder what could be going on and if he actually was in some sort of trouble. Halle twisted her hair around her finger continuously in worry. Before her law class began, she tried texting him again, but he never responded, increasing her panic.

She sat in her usual chair in the classroom on the second floor of the social sciences building, staring out the tiny rectangular window in hopes that, by some miracle, Alex would walk by, even though his next class took place in a building on the far side of campus. Halle swept her finger across her phone screen, the fifth time in as many minutes, checking again to see if she'd received anything from her boyfriend.

"Miss Henry?" Mrs. Monroe asked, causing Halle to look up. "Is something the matter?"

"No, ma'am."

"We've not heard from you yet today, which is a bit abnormal, to say the least. You are usually quite vocal when it comes to our political discussions."

Several students sitting around Halle snickered. True enough. What were they discussing, the Clean Water Act? Damn it, she always chimed in on that one.

"Um, actually . . ." Halle stalled, her hazel eyes pleading. "I'm not really feeling very well. I, I . . . think I should go see the nurse."

Mrs. Monroe blinked several times. "Okay."

Halle jumped from her seat, grabbed her backpack, and hurried out the door. If Alex wouldn't tell her what was going on, she'd find out for herself.

Sprinting across the quad, Halle ran toward the administration building. By the time she reached the school's main offices, she was out of breath. Panting, she unbuttoned her blazer, letting the cool air in, and sped up the back stairs toward Mr. Davies's office, not entirely sure what she would say if someone asked what she was doing.

Halfway down the hall, she spied Alex sitting in one of the three wooden classroom chairs placed outside the dean's office door. His hair stood on end, his elbows were on his knees, and his head was cradled in his hands. Her heart dropped.

Halle's breath caught in the back of her throat as she took in Alex's appearance. "Are you okay?" she asked, slowing her pace as she approached.

"No."

Halle lowered herself onto the chair next to him. "What's going on?" She placed her hands on the back of his neck and started to massage his tense shoulders.

"It's bad, Hal. They're kicking me out of school."

"What!" Halle's fingers stopped moving.

"They found a bag of pot in my book bag."

"Are you serious?"

"It's not mine. I told them it wasn't mine, that I had no idea how the stuff even got into my bag, but Davies doesn't believe me."

Halle thought of what Izzy said yesterday when they were walking into Campbell House. "It's Wyatt's, Alex. You need to tell Mr. Davies. Your sister told me that Missy said they were going to go smoke together this weekend. She's been bragging about it all over campus. Izzy can tell Mr. Davies that the weed is Wyatt's. This is just a misunderstanding."

"Hal, Wyatt's dry. You know he was kicked out of his last school for smoking pot. He hasn't smoked it since. The pot's not his."

"Bullshit. Missy said—"

"Listen to yourself, Halle. You're believing crap Missy said to my sister. You know they both love to gossip. I live with Wyatt. I would know if he were smoking anything. It's not something you can hide from your roommate. Besides, there are other reasons too, things I promised him I wouldn't tell anyone."

Halle cracked her knuckles, a nervous habit she picked up from her dad that she perfected since she knew the sound drove her mother nuts.

"Did they give you a drug test?"

"Yeah. It came back negative, but Davies doesn't care."

"What? How can he not care? He has to. The test proves you didn't do anything."

"I know, but he found the pot himself when he forced me to go through my bag in front of him. He said that the evidence was irrefutable. I don't know what to do, Halle."

"Where was it?"

"The front pocket. Here." Alex pointed to the narrow slot at the front of his messenger bag.

"But you never use that compartment. It's too narrow. You can't even fit a phone in there."

"I know, I told him that, but he wouldn't listen. The crap was even wrapped in this crazy wax paper bag. The kind my mum used to stick our sandwiches in back in elementary school. Where the hell am I supposed to get one of those around here?"

"But this is your first offence. Shouldn't you just be suspended or given work hours?"

"No. Technically, this is my second offence. Remember grade 9 when I walked into Kevin's room and the grade 12s were partying?" Alex buried his face in his hands. "My parents are going to kill me. My dad will never believe I didn't do anything."

"Yes, he will."

"No, Halle, he won't."

"Come on, Alex. He's your dad. He trusts you."

"Halle, he caught me and my friend Jack smoking pot two summers ago, down by the docks. I never told you because I was embarrassed.

Jack kept telling me I had to try it. We'd already had a couple beers so I thought what the hell. Just once. No one will know. I haven't even told Iz about it. Anyway, when Dad caught us he freaked. He said if he ever caught me doing drugs again my life was over. I'm screwed."

"Crap."

"Yeah."

Halle straightened her back. "Alex, we have to fight this. That isn't your pot. This isn't right!"

Alex looked down. "Mr. Davies already called Mum and Dad. They're on their way to campus. Shit, Hal, you know my dad. He'll listen to Mr. Davies and if the school says I did something, my dad will think I did too."

"Can't Mr. Scott do anything? He's your dorm father, he knows you would never do anything like this."

"From what I overheard when he and Mr. Davies were talking on the phone, he tried, but Davies isn't budging."

"But what about school, college, your future? They can't kick you out. We're about to graduate!"

"Since my test was clean they can't charge me with anything but possession," Alex said. "I can finish up my classes at home. Mr. Davies said I'll still be able to graduate. I'm just not allowed back on campus. I don't know what the universities I applied to are going to say. If I can't row with the team, though, I can kiss my dream of getting a scholarship to the University of Washington goodbye."

"Oh my God." Halle sighed, the weight of the situation squeezing the air from her lungs.

"I know."

Halle buried her head into Alex's neck.

"Mr. Scott is on his way to escort me back to the dorm so I can pack up my things. He should be here any minute. As soon as Mum and Dad get here I have to leave."

CHAPTER 20

Halle's heart sank as she stood on the grass watching the Dumas's car pull away from Lockhart House, the dorm Alex had lived in for the last four and a half years. The dark green Ford Explorer wove through the school's drive out to the main road. Its taillights vanished behind the bend, leaving Halle staring at the yellow line used to separate oncoming traffic.

"This is not right." The gray clouds overhead reflected her mood. Halle felt a tear trickle down her cheek. She had tried not to cry earlier, but now that Alex was gone she couldn't help it.

Izzy shivered next to her. "I don't think I've ever seen Dad so mad. I can't believe Alex never told me about smoking up before."

"Iz, you can't tell anyone about that."

"I know and I won't. But you know how old-fashioned Dad is, how seriously he takes drinking, drugs, and our education. He'll take Alex getting busted as a personal insult and probably blame him for sullying the family name."

"Do you really think your dad would do that?"

"Yeah, did you see him? Everything between his big Greek nose and the bald spot on the back of his head was red. He was six feet of pissed off. He probably won't stop yelling at Alex until they get home."

"I wish he'd listen to his own son. Alex didn't do anything." Halle sniffed. "I need to make this better. This isn't how our senior year is supposed to end."

Izzy reached for her roommate's hand. "Are you going to be okay?"

Halle toyed with the zipper on her black school raincoat, frustration replacing sadness. "I'm going to bring Alex back to school, Iz. I'm going to make this right. What happened to your brother is wrong. That wasn't his pot they found."

Halle looked up at the three-story Tudor boys' house behind her. Within the hour students would be heading to Mason Hall for their evening meal. Answering people's questions about what just happened felt like the last thing Halle wanted to do.

"Think Mrs. M will excuse us from dinner tonight?" Izzy said, reading Halle's mind. "I don't feel very social."

"Me neither," Halle said. "Let's ask."

"Here, wait a second. I'll text her."

The light in Alex's room turned on, second from the right, third floor, at the front of the building. Halle knew the window well. Wyatt opened the blinds.

"Alex said the pot wasn't Wyatt's, but I'll bet money it was."

"What did you say?" Izzy asked, pulling Halle away.

"Nothing," Halle growled.

"Crap, I think it's about to rain. Hurry up," Izzy said, as the first big drop crashed to the pavement.

"I'm coming." Halle looked up at the heavy cloud cover. "Really? You do know how cliché it is that you're starting to rain right now?"

Tasting her salty tears on her lips, Halle wiped her cheek with her cuff and fell in step with Izzy.

"All I want to do is make a bunch of Top Ramen, watch a movie, and eat candy till I feel sick," Izzy said, opening the door to their dormitory.

Halle slumped. "This sucks."

"Yeah, it does."

"But, Iz—"

"Halle, stop right there. You can't go on like this. I know you want to be all sad. I can even guess what you're about to say. I love him too. But he wouldn't want you to feel like this."

Halle nodded, the words she'd been about to speak sticking in her throat. Her feet felt heavy, like her shoes weighed one hundred pounds each.

Izzy stood on her toes and wrapped her arm around her roommate. "Let's go eat chocolate."

Thankful that the dorm appeared vacant, Halle trudged up the stairs.

Izzy's phone dinged as it received an incoming message. "Mrs. M says we have permission to stay here all night. She said she'd have Kelsey sign us in, so we don't even have to leave the room."

"Thank God. Right now I swear I might kill the first person that says something about Alex."

"Yeah, me too."

Halle sank into the pillowy warmth of her bed. "I feel so lost."

"Here." Izzy passed Halle her favorite pair of thick navy sweatpants with the store's label "ROOTS" printed across the bum. "Change into these and find a cheesy '80s movie on Netflix. I'm going to boil some water for the noodles."

"Izzy?" Halle called out as her roommate walked from the room.

"Yeah?"

"I love you."

"Love you too, roomie."

"Thanks."

CHAPTER 21

Halle was deep in a dream when the alarm on her phone sounded, waking her. The door to the bathroom they shared with the two girls living in the room next to them flew open, a bouncing, freshly showered Izzy emerging.

"Come on, lazy butt," Izzy said, grinning.

"How can you be smiling?"

"Easy. It's a beautiful day. Check out the blue sky." Izzy spread the curtains wide, letting in the bright sunlight.

"I'm going to kill you," Halle moaned, clutching her pillow to her eyes.

"Alex texted me a couple minutes ago. They got home okay. He said he's grounded like forever."

Halle groped for her phone. There were three messages from Alex, all saying about the same thing.

"Come on, Hal, get up. Let's go grab something to eat before class."

"I'm not hungry. You go." Halle's stomach growled, betraying her.

"Not going to work."

"Okay, fine, I am hungry. I just don't feel like facing the gossip mill in Mason. Not yet. Give me the morning. I have a box of Pop-Tarts in my lock drawer under my bed. I'll eat those. Go meet Jacob. I know he's waiting for you."

A slight grin spread across Izzy's face. "I know I shouldn't be this happy right after my brother's been expelled, but being with Jacob just makes me smile."

"Okay, there's reason number two why I don't want to go down to breakfast."

"You sure?"

"Yeah."

Halle dragged her hand down her face. She lay there thinking for fifteen minutes before slowly pulling herself out of bed and making the trip across the room to her closet. She cared little what she looked like. With Alex gone she didn't even care if she brushed her hair. Maybe she'd forget to brush her teeth. Would anyone notice?

Moaning, she grabbed a wrinkled dress shirt from her closet floor. "Well?" she mumbled, brushing dirt from the collar. "Guess this is better than nothing." To her right she spotted her crumpled skirt lying across the back of her desk chair. Thank God they had a uniform, she thought, otherwise she'd probably just stay in pajamas.

The corner of her phone caught her eye as the device vibrated on her desk with an incoming text.

•

April 9, 2015 8:10 AM

Izzy: You out of bed???

> **Halle:** Yeah

Izzy: Promise?

> **Halle:** What are you, my mother?

Izzy: No, but I know you & your mood swings :P Plus I swore to Alex I'd get you to class. He's worried about you. Says you can't live without him.

> **Halle:** Piss off Iz

Izzy: :p

•

Checking her clock, Halle grabbed her books. Only ten minutes till class started. It took at least that long to walk to her classroom. The Pop-Tart would have to wait. The sugar would only upset her stomach anyway. After class she'd grab a bagel or some kind of fruit juice drink from the student center.

The brisk morning air felt like a slap against her exposed cheek.

Halle shivered as the sun touched the back of her dark blazer, warming her slightly. Ahead of her, a group of boys emerged from Lockhart.

"You! Wyatt!" Halle yelled, spotting Wyatt amongst them. Her pulse quickened. "Stop right there!"

Wyatt excused himself from his friends and walked toward Halle. "What?"

"Alex getting kicked out of school is your fault!"

Anger surged through Wyatt's body. "Screw you."

"We both know that was your pot, not Alex's," Halle yelled, jamming her finger into his chest.

Wyatt clenched his hands, his slate-colored eyes reflecting the same hatred he saw in Halle's hazel ones. He stiffened, straightening so that he appeared taller, even though they were roughly the same size. The air between them stilled.

"Prove it."

"I intend to."

CHAPTER 22

Class sucked. School sucked. Everything sucked. Halle threw her book bag onto her unmade bed. "Great," she growled as her red pack bounced from the bed onto the floor, scattering her schoolwork across the room. Halle reached for the bottle of water resting on her desk and drank deeply. She paced, gulped, and paced some more.

Halle leaned against the edge of her desk, surveying the mess on the floor, then closed her eyes, trying to calm down. "Goddamn gossipmongers," she cursed.

The rumors were flying, and during the course of the day she heard that Alex had been expelled for dealing drugs, smoking crack, stealing, and, her personal favorite, having sex in the crew house with a grade 8.

The last one made her skin crawl for several reasons but mostly because she and Alex had been going out for over two years. They were rarely seen apart. The thought of someone saying he cheated on her made her want to hurl. Halle rolled her fingers into her palm, cracking each knuckle, pinky to thumb. People sucked.

Her phone buzzed.

•

April 9, 2015 3:20 PM

Alex: Hey, babe :)

    Halle: Hey! How are you?

Alex: There :/ Parental units are only allowing me to talk with you & Iz. I'm grounded for the rest of the month. He won't even look at me when I say I didn't do anything. He says he already caught me once and that the pot was found in my bag so I must have known about it, end of subject.

    Halle: That bites!!!

Alex: Totally

> **Halle:** At least he's letting you talk to me. :)

Alex: <3 How was your day?

> **Halle:** Awful. I hate being here without you. People
> are saying the stupidest things. Iz caught Missy
> telling people you were sent to rehab & someone's
> saying you slept with a grade 8.

Alex: What??? Sick! Dad did threaten to send me to rehab though.

> **Halle:** But you've only smoked once and haven't
> touched anything else.

Alex: I know that & you know that but Dad thinks otherwise.

> **Halle:** This is so messed up!

Alex: I know.

> **Halle:** I hate hearing people talk about you.
> Especially when they don't know anything.

•

Halle rolled her head, taking several large cleansing breaths while she waited for Alex's reply. Her heart felt empty. She sat on her bed, listening to the other girls returning from class, doors slamming, music blaring, and wondered if she'd ever feel normal again.

•

Alex: Anything new in class today?

> **Halle:** Missy got caught swapping spit with your
> roommate in the hall before AP lang.

Alex: Nasty.

> **Halle:** Those two are perfect for each other. Both
> losers. Missy keeps telling people they're still going
> to party hard this weekend. I'll bet money the pot in
> your bag is Wyatt's! Think about it. He could have
> heard someone coming, panicked & stashed the bag
> in your pack. The thought has to have crossed your

mind. Doing something like that would be just like him.

Alex: Halle, he's dry.
Back off! Missy's full of it. She's just
trying get attention.

        Halle: I'm right about this Alex. He would easily put his future before yours.

Alex: Seriously Hal.
I know him way better than you do. Back off.

April 9, 2015 3:32 PM

Alex: Hal…
Alex: Please, I don't want to fight.

        Halle: I don't want to fight either. But you need to listen to me on this. You should hear the things people are saying around here. If I can get Wyatt to confess to putting his drugs in your pack, you can come back & this will all be over.

Alex: Listen, Mum's yelling at me to come down and help with dinner. I have to go. But trust me. This isn't Wyatt!

        Halle: Yes it is!

Alex: No it's not!!!

        Halle: How can you be sure?

Alex: I just am. Trust me on this. Please. I love you.

        Halle: Whatever.

•

Halle drained the last of the water from her bottle and wiped her lips dry with the back of her hand. She needed ChapStick in a bad way. She got up from the bed and went over to her desk. Old assignments littered the surface.

She couldn't understand this. Alex refused to believe that the drugs that got him expelled could have been Wyatt's. Why? The idea of someone walking around campus free while Alex sat at home taking the blame for something he didn't do made her want to scream. If only she could prove the pot wasn't his, the school would have to bring him back. Things could go back to the way they were. Then she and Alex would be together again.

Halle reached for her laptop and pressed the Power button. Two new emails regarding homework assignments lit up her campus inbox. Halle drummed her fingers across her desk—*click, click, click . . . click, click, click . . .* She needed to get Alex back to Lakeview before she went crazy. An Amazon.com advertisement for The Spy Shop appeared in the sidebar of her news feed.

"Oh my God," Izzy announced, throwing open their door. "Miss Cramer sucks! If I have to listen to one more of her lectures on the anatomy of the frickin' salmon I am going to puke!"

Halle moved the curser over the advertisement and pressed Enter.

"Halle Henry, are you listening to me?" Izzy demanded, slamming her pack down on the window seat.

Halle sighed. "Iz, I'm in the middle of something here."

"Well then, stop. I need to bitch or I'm going to be a bitch. Then, I need you to tell me what to wear when I meet Jacob later."

"Iz, Miss Cramer's a biology teacher. What do you expect? It's her job to teach you about reproductive systems."

"I know, but she said I used the dissection knife improperly. I cut the damn thing open. Isn't that what counts?"

"Do you want me to help you? I could go over your notes with you.

I got an A in the course last year."

"Show off."

Halle chuckled.

"Are you laughing at me?"

"Maybe."

Izzy dug into her closet, pulling out a loud red T-shirt and a pair of black skinny jeans. "Does this say slutty or cool?"

"I don't think Jacob's going to care what you wear, Iz," Halle said, sneaking a peek at her screen. "He's totally into you. You could go out in overalls and he'd still want to kiss you. Trust me."

Wrapping her tangled hair into a sloppy high bun, Halle scanned the page, pressing on the tab reading "Surveillance Equipment."

Q-See Surveillance Pen: a pen, a camera, a video recorder with three extra ink cartridges $40.00

Halle pressed the Add To Cart button. Scrolling farther down the page, Halle spotted her next item: Real-Time Live Mini Micro GPS Tracker. If Wyatt wouldn't admit to the drugs, Halle would have to prove they were his on her own.

"When Missy told you about her weekend plans, did she say where they planned on going or what time?"

"No, but OH MY GOD did you see them making out in the hall this afternoon?"

"So wrong!"

CHAPTER 23

An hour later, Halle was still crouched at her desk. She stood up and stretched, bending down to touch the floor, letting her back release. The tight brown carpet beneath her feet needed vacuuming. Old bits of chips along with crumbs from the cookies they ate the other night stuck to her toes.

She thought she had better text her mom before the charges for the spy stuff appeared on her credit card. She grabbed her phone and flopped onto her bed. Halle swore Lili checked the statements at least once a week. Best to avoid the inquisition.

April 9, 2015 10:05 PM

Halle: Hi Mom

      Lili: Hi Sweetie. How was your day?

Halle: AWFUL

      Lili: Sorry. Alex? Or is something else going on?

Halle: No, just Alex. I really miss him.

      Lili: :(

Halle: I ordered a couple things for school from Amazon today. I hope that's ok.

      Lili: Sure. What did you get?

Halle: Nothing much. Just stuff.

      Lili: You want me to call the grocery store and order chocolate cake for the house? Cake is good when you're feeling down.

Halle: Thanks Mom, but I'm not grade 8 anymore. Besides I don't want to get fat.

      Lili: You are far from fat Halle, but it's your call.

Halle: How's Dad?

> **Lili:** Good, sleeping, but you know him. Uncle Duncan has him working away. :) Do you want me to wake him? So you can say hi?

Halle: No, sorry. I should probably go. I've got a dorm meeting in 5. Sorry if I woke you up. I know it's pretty early there.

> **Lili:** Don't worry, I was up. You know me. I never sleep once the sun's up.

Halle: No, you never sleep when you have a good book. What time did you wake up?

> **Lili:** About an hour ago. Such a good book though. You're going to love it.

Halle: Can't wait. Send it to me when you're done and I'll start it the next time I fly home.

> **Lili:** Sleep tight love bug. If you need anything else just let me know. I love you.

Halle: Love you too! Give Dad a kiss.

> **Lili:** Will do -xoxo

.

Reluctantly, Halle felt herself smile. Offering to buy the house a cake was so like her mother, the comfort food queen. She'd probably send up a bunch of ice cream, too. Halle hated not being completely honest with her about what she was buying. Anyway, she wasn't really lying, right? Just not telling the whole truth.

CHAPTER 24

San Lucio, Tamura

Lili's arms prickled with goose bumps. Call it mother's intuition. Lili knew her daughters well enough to know when something was wrong. A few days ago, Halle called in tears when she found out her boyfriend was being expelled from school. Then last night, she hadn't answered any of her calls, only the texts this morning, saying she needed something for school but not saying what. That wasn't like her. Usually Halle told her more than she ever needed to know. Something had to be going on. One day Lili would make good on her threat to take away Halle's phone if she didn't answer so she could hear her voice, but not today. She looked back down at her phone's screen, her forehead creasing as she scowled.

"What happened?" Graham said sleepily, opening his eyes to look at his wife.

Lili yawned. Only 7:10 a.m. She hated the time difference between western Canada and Europe. "It's Halle."

A knowing look crossed Graham's face. "She still upset?"

"Yeah, but I think it's more than that. She's acting aloof, and you know how that bothers me."

"She's a teenager. Don't worry so much. She'll get over whatever this is soon enough. Maybe call Blakely. Have her check in with Hal tomorrow."

Lili nodded. "Good idea."

"Now get over here and give me a hug. I still have twenty minutes before I have to wake up."

Lili turned toward her husband of twenty-eight years, shaking her head, making Graham snort.

"Everything is going to be okay, Mom. Stop worrying so much."

Graham pulled Lili into his arms, kissing her.

•

April 10, 2015 11:03 AM

Lili: Morning love

    Blakely: Hi Mom.

Lili: How's your day going?

    Blakely: Good, about to go to world economics.

    How's yours?

Lili: Good. Dad & Uncle Duncan started working on the new recycling laws yesterday. I'm worried about Hal though. She's not answering my calls. Only texting. Could you ring her?

    Blakely: Sure. What's up?

Lili: She sounds a bit off.

    Blakely: What do you expect? She's probably going

    through hell right now. :(

Lili: I know. I just would feel better if you'd talk to her. You know me…

    Blakely: LOL, yes Mom.

Lili: Thanks love

    Blakely: You're pathetic. :)

Lili: I know, but I love you guys.

    Blakely: Haha -love you too <3

Lili: :)

CHAPTER 25

Lakeview Academy

The grassy lawn in front of Campbell House glowed green. Seriously green. Everything on campus took on the surreal color this time of year—lakes, trees, even the moss on the roofs—because of the heavy rainfall and moderate temperatures on Vancouver Island. The place seemed like a bloody jungle for more than half the year.

Halle's stomach lurched. Turning away from her window, she poured a handful of Tums onto her desk and picked out the yellow ones, plopping two of them on her tongue. Izzy liked the red Tums best, so she saved those for her. In the three days since Alex left she'd only left her room for classes and sport, her anxiety over his predicament taking its toll on her.

The school still buzzed with inaccurate accounts of what happened. Talking to people in order to straighten out the rumors seemed pointless. They were going to believe what they wanted to believe, regardless of the truth.

Halle combed her tangled hair with her fingers while gnawing on her lower lip, now cracked and shredded to the point of bleeding. She couldn't believe what they'd served for lunch. So. Not. Chicken. Thank God she had a spare class next so she could lie down in her room to allow her stomach to settle before going to her next class.

Her computer's iChat alarm rang with an incoming call, startling her. She hurried from the window seat she'd been sprawled across to press the connect icon.

Alex's unkempt face glowed to life on the screen. Several days worth of stubble covered his cheeks, making his chin even more pronounced than usual. Since his parents grounded him they had only communicated through text messages. Actually seeing him in his room now made her want to cry all over again. Quickly wiping the corners of her eyes with the end of her untucked shirt, Halle turned her video on.

"Hal?"

"Here!"

"Hey."

"Hey yourself."

Halle swallowed hard. Heavy dark circles still shadowed Alex's usually worry-free eyes. "How are you?"

"Truthfully, not so good. Mum's constantly harping on me about how drugs can mess up your life, Dad rarely looks in my direction without shaking his head, even Dexter won't hang in my room, and he's *my* damn dog. No matter how many times I tell them I didn't do anything they still don't believe me. Do you know how much it sucks to have your own parents refuse to consider that you just *might* be innocent? It's messed up, that's what it is. Then to top things off I hate that we're in a fight. I can't even be there to explain my reasoning for trusting Wyatt in person."

"I know. I don't like fighting with you either." Halle took in the room behind him. It didn't seem that long ago that she had been there. After Christmas in Tamura she'd flown back to Canada to spend New Year's Eve with his family in Tofino. They'd built a big bonfire on the sandy beach, huddling with friends in the clear frigid air, and partied until the horizon started to glow. Halle remembered Alex holding her hand as they watched the sunrise together, making plans for their graduation. She did a double take as she noticed an old photograph still taped to his wall.

"Hey, I thought I told you to take down that picture of me," she said, pointing.

Alex looked behind him at the image he captured of Halle back in their grade 8 photography class and grinned. "I never said I'd take that down. I like it. You look cute."

"I look gross! God, Alex, we weren't even dating yet. I'm wearing my retainer."

"My room, my rules; picture stays."

Halle's smile reached her eyes for the first time in days. "Fine, but don't forget all the old pictures in my arsenal. When you get back here, you're dust. I'm pasting them all over the Lockhart common room."

Alex looked at the photos on the wall and sighed before turning back to face her. "Hal, I'm not coming back. You need to accept that this is it."

"Don't say that!"

"I'm just looking at the facts. I didn't get suspended. I got expelled. I'll be lucky if I get into community college now."

"But Mr. Davies said if you keep up with your courses you'll graduate with the rest of us. You're just not allowed back on campus."

"Yeah, but Dad keeps insisting that no university will take me now that the expulsion will show up on my final transcript. I don't know what to believe anymore."

"He's just upset, Alex. That's not going to happen. You'll get accepted somewhere, I know it."

"Yeah, but I've dreamt of rowing for the University of Washington since I was a kid. Hal, they just won their fifth national championship. That's not going to happen now that I'm off the team. Plus I need a scholarship in order to attend an American university. Who's going to give me one of those now?"

"Then we have to get you back to campus, Alex. I'll prove the drugs were Wyatt's and you'll get into the UW like you've always dreamed."

Alex's voice dropped. "Jesus, Halle, give up this stupid thing with Wyatt, *please*. How many times do I have to tell you: Wyatt didn't plant the drugs in my pack! I've always left my books lying around. Anyone could have stuck the pot in there. Lay off Wyatt! His life has been shit. He's the last person on earth who deserves your wrath."

"What do you mean my wrath? And how do expect me to lay off if you won't even tell me why you're so sure it wasn't him in the first place."

Halle could see the veins bulge in Alex's neck. "Halle, we both know how obsessed you can get when you think you have something to prove. I lived with Wyatt all year. Trust me. I know he's not responsible for this. He doesn't talk about what he's going through, but I know he's not doing drugs."

"How can you be so sure?"

"Jesus." Alex wrung his hands together. "If I tell you why I know, will you promise not to say anything and leave him alone?"

"Yes."

"His mother makes the school give him weekly drug tests. Her new husband insists she do it because he doesn't like Wyatt. He's some sort of minor-league politician with lofty goals who thinks Wyatt is nothing but a liability. That's why his mother packed him up and sent him away."

"But didn't he get booted from his last school for doing drugs?"

"Yeah, he was a partier. After his dad died he got really depressed and started hanging out with the wrong people. But he only got suspended from his old school, not expelled. His mum just didn't want to deal with him anymore, that's why he's at Lakeview."

"His dad died?"

"Yeah."

"How?"

"In a car accident. Wyatt was with him. He was twelve."

"Seriously?"

"Wyatt spent four months in the hospital after the crash. His father was killed instantly. Like I said, Wyatt didn't care what happened for a long time after that, but now he does. He wants to make his dad proud and be a lawyer like he was. His stupid mother doesn't even care that he's getting good grades now or that he's been clean for nearly two years. He's already been accepted to Duke, Halle. He never wants to go back to Toronto or his mother again, and now that I know what it's like to have your parents not believe you, I don't blame him."

Halle closed her eyes, hating how wrong she was. Seconds passed, feeling like minutes. If Wyatt hadn't been the one to put the drugs in Alex's pack, then who did?

"Seriously, that's messed up."

"So will you back off now?"

Sheepishly, Hale nodded. "Yes."

Halle heard Alex's mother call his name.

"I gotta go. I'm glad we got to talk, though." Alex touched his lips and blew Halle a kiss. "Remember, don't say anything. Not even to my sister. Promise?"

"Promise."

"I miss you."

Halle sighed. "I miss you too."

Alex's hand drifted to his keyboard. "Bye."

The screen went black. Halle thought about having to take weekly drug tests. She couldn't imagine her parents ever treating her like that. For the first time since Alex and Wyatt became roommates, Halle felt sorry for Wyatt.

CHAPTER 26

Fat tears raced down Halle's cheeks. Alex really wasn't coming back. She'd been so sure she could prove his innocence, that soon this whole nightmare would be over. She buried her face in her hands.

Halle threw her head back, glancing at the Spackle patterns on the ceiling. She hated when she was wrong about something or someone. God, apologizing to Wyatt would be brutal. She knew she needed to, though, for Alex, if nothing else. Crawling onto her bed, she curled into a ball and closed her eyes.

Two hours later, Mrs. Middleton knocked on her door. "Halle?"

The alarm clock next to her bed glowed 3:05. Halle rubbed her eyes. "Come in."

"I got a message telling me you didn't attend your last two afternoon classes."

"Sorry, I guess I fell asleep during my spare."

Mrs. Middleton noticed the trail of mascara dripping down Halle's cheek. "Are you all right, dear?"

"Yes, I'm fine. I'm just really tired. I haven't been getting much sleep."

Having been a houseparent for over ten years, Mrs. Middleton knew what Halle must be feeling. This wasn't the first time she had witnessed a girl's boyfriend expelled. The heartbreak of any child being removed from school always weighed heavily with the staff. "Well, I'll have your teachers excuse your absence, but I want you to go to tutorials next week. And promise me you'll get some rest this weekend."

"Thank you," Halle said, relieved.

Satisfied that she had eased at least a little of Halle's strain, Mrs. Middleton left.

Halle pushed away her duvet, yawning. Sport practice would start in an hour. She should probably start working on the classwork she missed. Her heart hurt, though. Accepting the fact that Alex might never come back seemed too much for her mind to take in. She didn't want their relationship to end this way. She knew that she and Alex weren't like her sister and Max; they most likely were not in the one percent that went on after high school and ended up getting married. She wanted to go to university in Europe, and he dreamed about attending school closer to home, in the United States. She just expected they'd still have at least the next three months together.

CHAPTER 27

"I'm going to go meet Jacob after prep. Do you want anything from the student center? Smoothie, gummies, chocolate?" Izzy asked.

"No."

"Come on, Hal, you've got to eat something. You've been in our room since your spare. And you look like crap. Come with me even. I'll wait. Just don't keep moping around here like this. If you don't snap out of this funk, Mrs. Middleton will call in the school counselor."

"She probably already has," Halle grumbled, pushing the tangled mound of hair from her face. "Fine. I'm not going out, but if you want to grab me a strawberry smoothie I'll drink it."

"Good!" Izzy pawed through her closet. "Can I borrow your blue sweater?"

Halle rolled her eyes. "Yes." Even if she and Alex couldn't be together anymore, at least she had Izzy.

Halle's phone lit up with an incoming call.

"Is that my brother?"

Halle smiled. "Yeah."

"Tell him hi."

Halle picked up her phone. "Hello?"

"Holy crap. You are not going to believe what I just saw when I was helping Mum do the dishes."

"I'm out of here," Izzy said, waving goodbye.

Have fun, Halle mouthed. "What?" she said to Alex.

"Have you seen a copy of today's *Victoria Times Colonist*?"

"No."

"Go get one, seriously. Like right now. The guy I saw getting shot is on the front page!"

"Excuse me?"

"I'm not making this up. I swear the guy on the cover of today's paper is the guy I saw on the ferry! He's some big drug dealer from Florida. Been missing for weeks. The paper says his parole officer tracked him to Vancouver and that he was last seen on the goddamn ferry we took. I'm telling you, Hal, I'm freaking out!"

"Oh my God!"

"I know. This is crazy. Have you talked to your uncle again? Did he say anything about this guy? Nico Soto. That's what the paper is calling him. Your uncle Mike's got to know about it. The article said the local police are involved. They even listed the West Vancouver Police number for people to call if they know anything. There's even a report about an abandoned car on the same boat a couple pages after the article, too, but nothing linking them."

"Are you sure?"

"Yeah! Google it if there isn't a copy around."

"Did you tell your parents?"

"Hell no, they'd probably make me go to the police and the police would want to know why I'm not in school. Then they'd find out about the pot in my bag. I'm already in enough trouble here at home. I don't need the police on my back too."

"Okay, give me a couple minutes to look this up. I'll call you back as soon as I've read both articles."

Just as Halle put her phone down it started ringing again. A picture of Blakely sitting on Max's lap appeared on the screen. They were dressed in shorts, laughing at a joke she had just made when Halle snapped the photograph, saving it as her sister's contact image.

Irritated by the distraction, Halle picked up her phone. "Hey, Blake," she said, quickly typing in the web address for the largest newspaper serving Vancouver Island while she talked. "Can I call you later? I'm wicked busy right now."

"Hey yourself, Hal."

"Seriously, I'm in the middle of something here." Halle didn't have time, nor did she want to have a conversation with her sister at the moment. Sometimes Blakely just made her feel like her problems didn't matter. She couldn't handle that right now. Not with what Alex just told her.

"Well, you don't have to be a brat about it."

Halle rolled her eyes. "Sorry, I'm just super distracted right now."

"You promise you'll call back? Mom's freaking out. She wants to know if you're doing all right."

"Ughhh," Halle groaned, throwing her head back. "Seriously? Tell her I'm fine."

"You sure about that?"

"Yes. Like I said, I'm just busy. Can I call you tomorrow, please, when I have more time?"

"Don't forget."

"I won't."

"Love you, sissy."

"Whatever."

Blakely laughed, making Halle smile, then hung up.

The first article Alex referred to pulled up immediately. A full-color picture of a dark-skinned man with a closely trimmed head of black hair, a thin mustache, and a narrow chin patch stared back at her. Something about the mug shot made her shiver. If this Soto guy was last seen on the ferry with them, why didn't her uncle say something? Halle thought she should have offered him the chocolates her mom sent after all; then maybe he would have followed through with her.

She typed Nico Soto's name into the search bar at the top of her screen. Seventy-three hits, all crime related, ranging from drug arrests to disorderly conduct to prostitution. From what she could gather from the various entries, Nico Soto was last seen in the West Vancouver area, boarding the Horseshoe Bay-to-Nanaimo ferry on the same day they'd been on board. Halle popped her knuckles. Uncle Mike would have known about Nico Soto's missing persons report days ago, maybe even before she told him about what Alex saw. Was that why he never called back? If the investigation had already started, he wouldn't be able to talk about it with her. Hence, his warning to her to stay out of it.

Frustrated, Halle clicked on several other links, trying to find a better picture of the man in question. Scrolling down the page she found a fuzzy photograph of a young Nico being arrested on the beach; the date on the image read 1998. A second man, being cuffed at the same time, looked away from the camera. Long black hair that reached his shoulders covered his face. Sweat stains soaked the front of his white tank top. On his exposed arm, Halle could just make out a tattoo stretching from his wrist to his elbow.

Halle copied the image, dragging the picture into her photo-editing program, where she enlarged the snapshot until she could make out the tattoo's details. Her whole body prickled. A serpent of red, black, blue, and yellow wrapped around the man's forearm. She'd seen that tattoo before. On Mr. Rivero.

"Holy crap," she said aloud.

Halle held her breath as she looked for more information on the early petty crime arrest, but there was nothing. No links, no names, no dates.

CHAPTER 28

Hot water eased the tension from Halle's neck. After hitting a dead end with her search, she'd given up. The man in the picture had hair. Mr. Rivero, none. Bald as a pickle, whatever that meant. But she couldn't shake the image of that serpent tattoo.

"I'm back," Izzy called into the bathroom. "I'll leave your smoothie on the counter next to your towel."

"Hey," Halle called out, stepping from the shower stall wrapped in a fluffy pale blue robe. "How did the date go?"

Izzy beamed. Halle thought she looked happier than she'd ever seen her.

"He asked me out, like to be his girlfriend. I can't believe how lucky I am! I'm pumped. I've never been someone's official girlfriend before."

"Cool, congrats!" Halle said, happy for her roommate.

"I know! Hook-ups and 'just hanging out' suck."

Izzy wetted her washcloth and started scrubbing the makeup from her face while Halle towel-dried her hair. They shared the sink and counter with the two other girls in the neighboring room, but each of them maintained a shelf of their own to store personal items and towels. Izzy put toothpaste on her Sonicare toothbrush. "How was your night?"

"Weird."

"What do you mean?" Izzy gurgled, her toothbrush buzzing.

"I'm not really sure where to start." Halle walked into their bedroom, crawled into bed, and brought her laptop down to her knees. "How do I spell Mr. Rivero's first name?" she asked.

"I think its Ramon: R, A, M, O, N. Why?"

"I just thought I'd do a quick Google check on him for Alex. The front page of the *Times-Colonist* has a picture of a missing drug dealer from Florida. Alex says the guy looks like the man he saw Mr. Rivero with on the car deck of the ferry the night we came back to school."

"No way!"

"Yup. See what I mean by weird?" Halle retyped his name. Immediately, several articles about the school hiring him popped up on the screen but nothing before then.

"No kidding. Do you think Mr. Rivero is really involved in this, then?"

"Yeah. I found this picture taken like seven years ago. This drug dealer guy was getting arrested with another guy who had Mr. Rivero's same tattoo. Look."

Halle swiveled her screen so Izzy could see.

"I don't know, Hal, that guy doesn't really look like Mr. Rivero. For starters, he has hair."

"I know, but he could shave his head."

"Maybe the tattoo is some sort of Cuban thing. There could be dozens of people with tattoos like that."

"Yeah, maybe."

"Finding anything else?" Izzy said, hanging up the last of the clothes piled on her bed.

"No."

"What about on the school site. Don't all staff members post bios?"

"Brilliant," Halle said, logging on to the Lakeview Academy home page.

•

Ramon and Lola Rivero: *Married in 1998, Lola and Ramon come to Lakeview Academy via the eastern coast of the United States. Both trained nutritionists, Lola and Ramon plan and prepare the balanced meals our students and young athletes need to succeed.*

•

"Ha, says here that he and his wife are trained nutritionists. His wife is the one who cleans the tables. She's always dancing around with her earbuds in, right?"

Izzy yawned and scooted under her blankets. "Yeah, love to know where they got their training."

CHAPTER 29

Everyone had an electronic trail. It didn't make sense that Halle couldn't find anything on the Riveros before they came to Lakeview. She rubbed her stiff neck and then typed in Nico Soto's name again using a different search engine, hoping to spot some kind of link between the two men. Maybe there'd be more on the early arrest picture she saw. Think, she told herself, tapping her finger against the side of her keyboard. Nico Soto on Facebook; Nico Soto on Twitter; Nico Soto on Vimeo; Nico Soto on LinkedIn; nothing. Frustrated, Halle frowned. The search page continued. More links to newspaper articles appeared.

•

Parolee disappears from ferry; Parole officers baffled when convicted American felon Nico Soto vanishes after being spotted boarding a BC ferry bound for Vancouver Island

•

Okay, Halle thought. This looked a little different from the brief article at the top of the search page; maybe there was something more to this piece. Sucking her lower lip between her teeth, she read on.

•

Nico Soto disappeared last month after being released from the Florida State Penitentiary after serving six years for drug-trafficking charges. His partner at the time, Ramon Perez, was said to have escaped with over 150 kilos of cocaine.

•

Halle's mouth fell open. She glanced over at Izzy, sleeping soundly, and typed Ramon Perez into the search bar. The screen fluttered with activity.

Halle looked at the clock. Almost midnight. Too late to call and risk someone hearing. Picking up her phone, she started texting Alex.

•

April 10, 2015 11:48 PM

Halle: OH MY GOD

    Alex: What?

Halle: I think our Mr. Rivero is actually a drug dealer named Ramon Perez, on the run from the Florida police.

    Alex: Who?

Halle: The guy you read about in the paper today - Nico Soto, his ex-partner.

    Alex: What are you talking about?

Halle: Ramon Perez & the guy you think went overboard, Nico Soto, were partners in a massive cocaine deal in Florida, like 6 years ago. The police busted them and this Perez guy went missing with 150 kilos of cocaine.

    Alex: Are you serious?

Halle: Yes, Google Ramon Perez. He has a full head of hair & a soul patch, but I swear it's Mr. Rivero. They have the same tattoo.

    Alex: Hold up. Let me take a look.

•

Alex took a deep breath. From his bed in another town, he swore he could hear the sound of Halle's brain swirling. Something in his own head started to scream. He clicked on the light next to his bed and reached for his laptop, watching it come to life as he lifted the screen.

•

April 11, 2015 12:07 AM

Halle: You still there?

    Alex: Yeah.

•

Alex's heart started pounding. He could see why Halle was trying to link what he saw on the ferry to what she found online, but he didn't want her getting carried away. He wasn't even sure anymore that the man he saw was Mr. Rivero. If he was wrong, Halle would be getting into trouble, and he didn't want anything happening to her when he couldn't be there to help her out.

•

Halle: So did you find Ramon Perez? Isn't the likeness unbelievable? Alex, I think you just totally solved like a 6-year-old mystery.

> **Alex:** Slow down, Hal. I doubt it's him. There's no way the school would hire a drug dealer.

Halle: What are you talking about??? Mr. Rivero could totally be Ramon Perez.

> **Alex:** Take the pictures to your uncle, but I think you're wrong.

Halle: Wait a minute. You're the one who thought the guy you saw with this Soto guy was the school cook. Why are you taking it all back now?

> **Alex:** Jesus, Halle, if the Riveros have all that coke & money why the hell would they be cooking at Lakeview?

Halle: I don't know. They could be hiding out? A School would be the perfect place to hide.

> **Alex:** Don't you think they'd pick someplace a little better, less wet, definitely warmer. You can't even prove the Riveros are from Florida.

Halle: Look at the pictures, Alex. It's him! It's all there. If I could prove Mr. Rivero *was* from Florida, then maybe we could solve this guy Nico's murder. Wouldn't that be something??? Best case scenario, you're validated in what you saw & the school gets a new cook. You might be home eating your mom's good food but I'm still here & you know how brutal the "food" is here.

> **Alex**: Halle, if what I saw was a drug-related murder we need to let your uncle handle the case. Tell him what you found then leave the whole thing alone for the police to deal with.

Halle: I am not calling Uncle Mike. He'll be pissed I'm even talking about this with you. He already warned me not to get involved if anything came from that night & according to the paper something definitely happened.

> **Alex:** Halle, if your uncle hasn't talked to you & you're too stubborn to call him, you should leave this alone.

Halle: Alex, you're the one who brought it up and had me look at the newspaper articles in the first place.

> **Alex:** HALLE!!! Call your uncle or drop it!

Halle: ALEX!!!

•

Exasperated, Halle turned off her phone. She wanted to throw something. If Izzy wasn't asleep she would scream. How could Alex not see the similarities between Ramon Perez and Mr. Rivero? They had the same tattoo, for God's sake. The image, still on her computer screen, seemed to pulsate in front of her. The connections between what Alex saw on the ferry and what she found on the Internet were more than just a coincidence, Halle was sure of it.

CHAPTER 30

Halle woke with a throbbing headache and wanted nothing more than to stay in bed for the rest of the day. Izzy hummed along to her alarm clock playing the weekly top twenty.

"Do you have any Advil?" Halle asked.

"Yeah. Here. You look like crap. What time did you go to sleep?" Izzy said, passing Halle two blue gel caplets.

"I don't remember."

"Come on, get out of bed. Let's go to breakfast. You'll feel better."

"No, I just want to sleep. It's Saturday, Iz."

"Fine, have things your way. Do you want me to sign you in so you don't have to go down? If I do, you owe me."

Halle pulled the covers back over her head. "You're the best, Iz."

"Okay, but you're missing out. The Windsor House girls are making waffles to raise money for their next house outing. Kelsey told me they were going to have whipped cream, chocolate chips, and strawberries!"

Halle's eyes shot open as her head popped back out over the top of the covers. "Are you serious?"

Izzy nodded.

"Okay, I take back what I said, you are not the best. I can't believe you almost didn't tell me. Give me a minute." Halle jumped out of bed and grabbed an old pair of navy yoga pants, a sweatshirt, and her UGGs. She finger-combed her hair, braiding it so that it hung over her shoulder. "Ready."

Outside, the ground still wet from last night's rain sparkled with the morning sun the thinning clouds decided to let through.

"Morning," Jacob said, bouncing up the front steps to meet Izzy. His sideways grin made Halle smile. To her left, Halle could see Wyatt leaving Lockhart with two of his housemates.

Halle closed her eyes, inhaling the spring morning. "Give me a second, I have to do something real quick."

"Don't, Hal," Izzy said, squeezing her arm upon seeing Wyatt. "Listen to my brother, for once. I know you don't like him, I don't either, but you were pretty hard on him yesterday. Even I felt bad for the guy."

Halle crossed her eyes in frustration and slid her arm from her roommate's grasp. "I know. That's why I need to go talk to him and apologize."

Wyatt and his friends started down the steps, heading toward the main buildings.

Izzy's eyebrow rose. "You're going to apologize?"

"Don't give me that look. I can do the right thing when I have to."

"What look?" Izzy grinned.

"Wyatt, wait!" Halle yelled. Wyatt's pace quickened. "Please!"

Wyatt stopped, his gray-blue eyes searching Halle's face. He nodded off his friends. "Why? What do you want now? Here to accuse me of some new crime? Fire away. Give me your best shot. Trust me, by now I've heard everything."

"I want to say I'm sorry."

Wyatt tilted his head to the side, stunned by Halle's admission. ". . . Right."

"You know, you could wipe that smug-ass look off your face. This isn't exactly easy for me," Halle said, growing annoyed. It already took everything in her to approach him in a friendly manner.

"Is this your idea of an apology?"

Halle balled her fists at her side. "No." The corner of Wyatt's lip curled up a little. Halle took a deep breath. "You swear you had nothing to do with the bag of pot they found in Alex's pack?"

Wyatt shook his head, starting down the stairs again.

"Wyatt, stop!" Halle called, reaching for his arm.

He jerked at her touch. "Alex is my friend, Halle. I don't screw my friends over."

"I shouldn't have accused you. It's just . . . I heard . . . Well, Missy told Izzy you guys were smoking up sometime this weekend. I thought maybe you hid your stash in Alex's bag, letting him take the fall, not you, when he was caught with it."

"You think that little of me? That would be a pretty shitty thing to do to a friend, let alone the guy I've been living with for the past year. News flash: we got along. I liked living with Alex."

"I know. I'm sorry. I just really miss him. It's just that it's not right that he got kicked out for something we all know he didn't do."

"Yeah, but thanks to your dramatics, half the campus now thinks I'm the dick who got him kicked out. Missy is full of crap, too. I don't smoke anymore, and if I did, I'm definitely not stupid enough to torch up on campus."

Halle took a deep breath. "That's what Alex said."

"Well, maybe you should listen to him."

"Yeah, he said that too."

Wyatt's mouth twisted into a tense smile.

CHAPTER 31

"Alex!" Elena Dumas yelled.

Alex moaned. He hated being at home. Especially alone without friends or his sister. His mother called him a second time.

Alex looked up from his desk. "Coming!" The images of Nico Soto and Ramon Perez pasted to his screen stared at him when his gaze returned. He'd been at his computer all morning, getting very little sleep after his fight with Halle. Her face hung on every wall in his room; so many memories, pictures, things to remember her by everywhere he looked. He felt horrible that he snapped at her, but he also knew she wouldn't listen to him otherwise.

He wanted to strangle his phone or, at the very least, smash it against the wall so he couldn't keep rereading the texts they'd exchanged, but if he didn't hurry downstairs his phone would be the least of his worries. Funny how he blamed the phone for his feelings of frustration with Halle rather than himself.

Halle just pushed him too far last night. He knew he started the whole "Mr. Rivero killed someone," but that was when he'd been at school and in control of the situation. Now that he sat in an empty house hours away from his friends, things were different.

Alex dragged himself down the stairs to the kitchen, where his mother was. Boxes of books for the local school's Reading Is Fundamental program sat on the antique oak dining table. She had helped organize the event for the last eight years.

"There you are. I need your help." His mother's dark hair was piled high on her head in a tidy updo while her olive skin appeared paler than usual for this time of year. She looked small and haggard. Things would be so much easier if both his mum and dad would just believe that the crap Mr. Davies found in his bag wasn't his. His drug test proved he wasn't using.

Both of his parents emigrated from Greece when they were young, his mother just eight years old. Alex could detect only the slightest accent in her voice, yet if his Ya-Ya was visiting, they would speak only in Greek. Alex could converse in the language as well; both his parents made sure of that.

They met in college at the Greek festival put on by the Greek Orthodox church near their university. His father, Milo, received a degree in finance and his mother one in history. They were married soon after, and Elena got pregnant almost immediately. She never worked after finding out they were expecting twins, choosing instead to stay home and raise Alex and Izzy. Milo went into banking and was now a vice president and manager at the local CIBC branch.

"Sure, what do you want me to do?"

"Will you organize these books into grade levels; picture books for grades K through one, young readers and some picture books for two through three, and then young readers and books for four through six? I've got to be there in an hour, and I'm totally unorganized."

"Sure."

"*Skata*," his mother cursed, working a soapy dishrag over a stain on her blue-and-white button-down shirt. "I swear, one of these days I will get through a morning without spilling coffee on myself."

Alex smiled. He never heard her swear in English, but Greek seemed to carry its own set of rules.

"Now I'm going to have to change my shirt." Elena threw her towel in the sink and stomped down the hall to the master bedroom, located at the back of the house on the main level.

Only Izzy and Alex slept in the bedrooms on the second floor. Another reason Alex felt so isolated. He didn't realize how noisy the dorms were until he was forced to sleep alone on an empty floor.

Alex brushed the hair from his eyes and started stacking the books in piles as his mother instructed. This time when Elena entered the kitchen, she wore a pink button-down and khaki slacks.

"When you're done, will you carry the books for the kindergarten and grade one classes to my car?"

"Sure."

"Why don't you come with me? I could use your help, and I'm sure you'd like to get out of the house."

"Isn't Dad going to think I'm trying to sell drugs to the little kids?"

"Now, Alex, don't you start with me. You are in trouble for a reason. The accusations against you are serious. There were drugs in your pack, and you have been caught with marijuana before."

"Mum, I smoked pot once, years ago, and for the last time, the drugs in my book bag were not mine! Why won't you guys believe me?"

"Alex, this subject is closed. You're just lucky the school is still letting you take online classes so you can graduate on time."

"The "accusations," as you call them, against me are bogus. I should be at Lakeview taking real classes."

"Enough. Just put the books in the car and stop arguing with me."

CHAPTER 32

After rowing, Halle sat on the bench overlooking the lake, next to the crew house. She liked this part of campus, especially when no one else was there. The maple trees around the lake were thick with new growth, changing the shoreline's winter brown to a stunning lime green. How did things get so messed up in her personal life, she wondered, burying her hands in her lap.

The lake's surface looked like glass. Not a ripple of wind. The dark color reflected the soft clouds drifting overhead. Just enough blue to make a man's pants, she thought, looking up at the sky, remembering her grandmother's favorite phrase about the weather this time of year. A mother goose with her five goslings swam past, honking loudly. The sun warmed her skin through her black lululemon tights. She toyed with her phone, looking at the recent photos friends had posted on Instagram, when it lit up with an incoming call.

"Hey, Hal," her sister bubbled through the other end of the line.

"Hi, Blake. Sorry I didn't call you back."

"No problem. As I said, Mom just wanted me to call and check in on you. Are you doing okay? Because if you are I have news, and I want you to be the first one I tell!"

"Yeah, I'm fine." Halle didn't want to drag her sister down by going into details about her fight with Alex. Blakely sounded too happy. All Halle would do is complain about her boyfriend not being on campus. Even she was tired of hearing herself whine. "Why? What's going on?"

"Will you be my maid of honor?"

Halle's whole body tensed with excitement "What!"

"Max just asked me to marry him!"

"Oh my God!" Halle touched her free hand to her lips, smiling.

"I know!"

"I'm so happy for you! Do Dad and Mom know?"

"He asked their permission over Christmas, I guess. I can't believe they didn't say anything."

Halle could hear the excitement in her sister's voice. "How did he ask you?"

"He picked me up this morning after classes and took me on a picnic to the bluff behind campus. Halfway through the meal, he got down on his knee. He had the ring in his pocket. I guess he's been carrying it around all week, waiting for the right time. He said he wanted to ask me before we went home for spring break, since that way we would have time to make an announcement before someone caught a glimpse of my ring and word got out to the press. We're thinking about a fall wedding. He wants North to be his best man. He's talking to him right now. So will you do it? Will you be my maid of honor?"

"Do you even have to ask? Of course I will. I'm so happy for you! What's the ring look like?"

"Here, I'll text you a picture. It's perfect! I guess Uncle Duncan said he should use one of the royal gems, but Max said no, he wanted to do the ring all on his own. He knew me before I was Queen, so he wanted something that would be ours alone, not royal, because to him, I'm still just Blakely, the girl he fell in love with. Isn't that sweet!"

Halle looked down at the image Blakely sent: a large oval-cut pink diamond surrounded by a circle of white diamonds set in rose gold on a thin, diamond-encrusted band. The ring couldn't be more perfectly suited for Blakely. Not too big or showy, but enough to look royal.

"Wow, I just got the picture. It's beautiful!"

"So me, don't you think? Mom helped him find the center stone. I didn't even know pink diamonds existed. I'm so happy. I guess I always knew we'd get married, but when he asked me I was completely surprised."

Halle talked to Blakely until the sun disappeared behind a cloud and she started to shiver.

"I have to go, Blake. I love you. And I am so excited for you guys. Give Max a big hug for me, promise?"

"I will. Stay strong, Hal. I'm thinking of you."

My sister's getting married. The thought filled Halle with joy, in spite of everything else going on in her life. At least there was something good to look forward to. Pocketing her phone, Halle went to find Izzy to tell her the news.

CHAPTER 33

Whoever invented Mondays should be shot. Halle glanced out the English building's second-floor window toward the lake. She watched the tops of the waves turn white, creating a pattern across the usually glass-like surface. She'd received word just after breakfast that rowing practice had been cancelled. The coach "highly" encouraged the team to go to the gym, but it wasn't required. Not until the fitness tests they had to take again on Thursday. Halle sucked her lower lip in. Normally, she and Alex would've gone into the village and bought food or just sat in the coffee shop, laughing at the newest round of outrageous campus gossip. Now, other people would entertain themselves with the rumors about them.

Not having Alex around campus felt unbearable. She tried texting Izzy to see what she was doing after class but got caught by the teacher. Now, her phone sat in a basket at the front of the room.

Halle closed her eyes and briefly slowed her breathing, wishing the second hand on the wall clock would speed up. She had called Alex yesterday to tell him about Blakely and Max. Luckily they hadn't fought again. Halle made sure not to bring up the subject of Mr. Rivero since Alex felt so strongly that she should leave things alone, refusing to see the similarities she did when comparing him to Ramon Perez. He was acting like she couldn't handle herself without him, which seemed utterly ridiculous and annoying as hell. The fact that her uncle left her out of the loop on what the police had discovered on the ferry made her angry as well.

Halle wrapped a piece of hair around her fingertip, holding it there until the end turned purple before unwinding the strand.

The class bell rang. Halle retrieved her phone from the basket and walked out the door. Izzy and Jacob were waiting for her in the hall.

"Hey, guys."

"You want to grab a cab and head into town with us?" Izzy asked. Halle noticed their intertwined fingers; an unwanted spike of jealousy pierced her heart.

"No, I think I'll head down to the library and help Mrs. M out. She probably needs some filing done."

Izzy's brows scrunched together in disbelief. "You sure?"

"Yeah. Thanks, though. I'd only bring you guys down." There was no way she wanted to be a third wheel with a new couple. If Alex were around, then being together would be fun, but seeing Izzy and Jacob kiss would just remind her of how alone she really was at the moment.

Halle looked down at her feet, toeing the tight gray weave of the commercial-grade carpeting they used in the classrooms with the worn tip of her black uniform flat.

"Want me to get you anything?" Izzy asked.

Halle could hear the hurt from her refusal in her roommate's voice. She would make it up to Izzy later, when they were alone in their room.

"No, that's okay. I'm getting better, though. I promise, by next week I'll be fine. You'll see."

"Alex would want you to still have fun, with or without him, Hal."

"I know."

CHAPTER 34

The library had gone through a major remodel during Halle's grade 8 year. The structure, still part of the main administration building, sat in the middle of campus. The addition of skylights let in tons of natural light while the continuance of brick siding on the outside blended the new modern wing with the older classic façade. Before the remodel, the library seemed creepy, but now the room felt warm, inviting even. Built-in pine cases filled with books lined the walls. The size of the school's book collection tripled after a major donation from one of the more successful alumni, a communications giant living in Ottawa.

Halle paused in front of the library's impressive new entry door, the six glass panels setting off a beautiful bronze door handle. She sometimes wondered if the old ghost stories from the days before the remodel would survive. She guessed they would, they were too good to forget altogether. Maybe the stories of Elsie, the ghost of the first headmaster's daughter, would change a bit, as all things do. Did anyone still hear the music box play after the library was closed? Did books still shut on their own or go missing only to end up on shelves where they didn't belong? She herself had seen nothing "abnormal" for years, although that hadn't always been the case. She missed her previous interactions with Elsie on occasion. Life with the school's most famous ghost had certainly been far from boring, taking up most of her first year at the academy.

Halle ran her hand down the bronze handle. Her chest felt heavy as it rose and fell with each new breath she took.

"Hey, Mrs. Middleton," Halle said, seeing her housemother as she pushed through the door. A couple of kids sat at tables dispersed around the open room.

Mrs. Middleton glanced up from her computer screen. "Halle? What can I help you with?"

After five years in Campbell House, Halle craved her dorm mother's smiling face as much as her own mother's. Recently, she heard rumors that Mrs. Middleton planned on retiring at the end of this school year. Her hair, more gray than black now, was the only thing to show the toll of years of service she'd given to the school. Halle wondered how many of the silver streaks were due to her sister, who lived her own adventures in Campbell House, and how many were caused by her.

"I was wondering if you needed any help? Practice got cancelled, and I didn't really feel like hanging around in my room by myself."

"No Izzy today?"

Halle laughed through her nose. "No, she and Jacob, the German exchange, are hanging out. I didn't want to get in the way."

"Isn't that nice. I'm glad our Izzy has finally found a good boy. I've heard nothing but positive things about him."

"Yeah, I'm really happy for her."

Mrs. Middleton looked over the top of her decorative reading glasses. "Well, I would certainly love the help. Never let it be said I turned a willing student away, especially if she's one of my own. There's a cart of books there that needs putting away."

Halle dropped her book bag behind the counter. "Sounds good."

Grabbing the handle of the pushcart, she started toward the bookshelves.

Lost in the titles, Halle barely noticed that over an hour had passed. When she finished, she returned to the desk, sitting to spin in Mrs. Middleton's leather chair. A hand stilled her movement, and Halle smiled at the unvarnished fingertips.

"If you are still looking for something to do, you can organize my desk drawer. I'm afraid it's gotten away from me a bit. I can't find a thing anymore."

Halle's nose wrinkled. "Can I still sit in your chair?"

Mrs. Middleton's soft laugh made Halle feel good about helping her out, instead of joining Izzy and Jacob like she kept thinking she should have. "Of course, but don't cause too much of a raucous; you'll disturb the other students."

Halle looked out at the now empty tables. "Don't think that's going to be a problem."

"Why don't you start by running down to the kitchen and grabbing some sandwich bags to put paper clips and the rubber bands in? There seems to be an abundance of them hiding in here."

Halle's eyes bulged as Mrs. Middleton pulled open the cluttered drawer. Oh yeah, she needed a whole box of bags by the look of things.

CHAPTER 35

"Hello?" Halle called out, pushing on the swinging doors to the kitchen. Timidly, she peered into the silent room. She thought for sure the kitchen would be full of people prepping food, with dinner less than two hours away. The thought of running into Mr. Rivero, or his wife, alone hadn't occurred to her until she saw the empty room. "Anyone here?"

Halle headed toward the far wall, eyeing the bank of drawers to the left of the oven. An industrial-size cling wrap sat on the stainless steel counter. Storage bags would have to be kept in the same area, wouldn't they, she hoped? Halle nervously cracked the knuckles on her left hand.

"You can't serve that!" she heard a woman yell.

"Like hell I can't!" came the reply.

Halle's breath caught in the back of her throat. "Crap, crap, crap, crap," she chanted, wishing she could find what Mrs. Middleton wanted someplace else on campus.

Quickly, she pulled open the top drawer: tinfoil, parchment paper, Saran wrap.

Lola pushed through the insulated doors separating the kitchen from the enormous walk-in refrigerator at the back of the room, a tray of frozen potato wedges in her arms.

"What do you want," she snapped, spotting Halle. "You aren't allowed in here. Get out."

"Um, sorry. Mrs. Middleton, the school librarian, sent me down here to grab a couple of small plastic bags for her."

Lola set down the tray. "Well, you're looking in the wrong spot," she barked, placing her right hand on her hip.

"Get your ass back here, Lola. I'm not done talking to you."

"Hold your horses, Ramon. We got company."

Ramon stomped into the kitchen. His cool gaze turned to Halle, making the hairs on the back of her neck stand up. "What the hell do you want, kid?"

Halle's voice hitched. "Plastic sandwich bags, please."

Ramon pointed a beefy finger toward the long stainless steel prep counter. "Under there."

"Thank you."

"In the plastic tub on top."

Halle nodded, removing the lid to the Rubbermaid bin.

"Grab what you need," Lola said, noticing the girl's hesitation.

Halle took in the contents of the three-by-two-foot container. There were several different sizes of resealable bags, but she stopped and stared when the thin box of waxed sandwich bags caught her eye.

"Jesus," Lola hissed impatiently, storming over to where Halle stood. "There're right here. You blind? How many do you need?"

Halle quickly grabbed several of the smaller bags, then one waxed.

"What do you want them for again?"

"Paper clips," Halle said, backing away. "Thank you."

CHAPTER 36

Lola watched the girl sprint from the kitchen after grabbing the bags, her brown ponytail swinging rapidly from side to side. Something about her seemed annoyingly familiar.

"*Mierda!*" Lola cursed. How did she not notice the resemblance before while the girl was standing in her kitchen?

"What," Ramon spat.

Lola turned to him. "You know who that kid was?" Her lip curled into a snarl as she extended her long finger to jab Ramon in the chest with the acrylic-tipped nail.

"No." The veins in Ramon's beefy neck bulged, pulsing from the sudden increase in his blood pressure.

"She's the girlfriend to the boy we just got kicked out."

"Whose girlfriend?"

"Of the kid who seen you off Nico."

Ramon groaned. "Lola, you said he was the only one who saw what I did. That the friends he told didn't believe him. You changing that now?"

"No, but I got a bad feeling that she just changed her mind about you. Did you see the look on her face when she left? Total panic. I'm telling you, something just set her off."

"What do you mean?"

"I mean, that girl—she couldn't get out of here fast enough once she got those bags. I think she's on to us too."

"Impossible. You think she's put everything together? You think she knows who we are? She might *think* I offed someone on the damn ferry 'cause of her stupid-ass boyfriend, but if she wasn't there she can't prove nothing and you know it. The boy's gone, woman. Leave it alone."

Lola walked over to the tub Halle had just been riffling through.

"Jesus Christ!" she shrieked, pulling out the box of waxed bags.

"What?"

Lola held the box over her head. "You goddamn moron, I told you to get rid of these!"

"I did. I put them in there so they'd get used up."

"I wrapped the marijuana I put in the kid's pack in one of these! Ten bucks says the kid told his girlfriend there what I did, and that's why she took off with that look. You idiot! When I say get rid of something I mean throw the damn things away. Don't just leave them lying around."

"Damn it, woman, why didn't you tell me?"

"I did, you dumbass," Lola snarled.

Ramon rubbed at the short hairs coming in above his temple where he'd shaved his head, something he did twice a day since arriving in Canada. "Now what?"

"I take care of the girl."

CHAPTER 37

Halle ran. She didn't care if she wasn't supposed to cut across the grass. Mud splatters stained her white knee-high socks. She headed for the boy's dormitory at the top of the hill, next to Campbell House, and took the stairs leading to the heavy double doors two at a time. Bursting through, she stopped.

"Halle?" Sarah Scott, Mr. Scott's wife, stood just inside the entry.

Halle leaned over, resting her hands on her knees, and took several deep breaths, struggling to fill her lungs with air.

Sarah adjusted the toddler on her hip, the younger of the couple's two children. "Is everything all right?"

"Yeah," Halle nodded. "I'm just looking for Wyatt."

"Wyatt?"

"Ha-ha," the toe-headed little girl squealed, extending her chubby baby arms to Halle.

"Hey, Teifi," Halle said, finally able to breathe normally. The baby's Welsh name tickled her tongue every time she spoke it, making her smile. At times, Halle swore Lakeview seemed more British than Canadian.

"I think Wyatt's upstairs, but I'm glad you're here. Can you babysit tomorrow night? Kennedy has been asking about you all week; she'll be sick she missed you when she gets home from school. Both girls haven't stopped talking about you and Alex since you two came over a couple weeks ago. Oh, honey, I'm so sorry about all that. How is he doing?"

"He's all right, and I'd love to come over sometime, Mrs. Scott. I'll check my calendar and text you if I'm free tomorrow."

Teifi wiggled from side to side in a desperate attempt to escape her mother's arms. "Down," she demanded.

"That would be great," Mrs. Scott said, clearly distracted.

"Down!" the toddler ordered again.

"Sorry, Halle, I need to get this little demon tucked in for a nap before she completely loses it. Say hi to Alex when you talk to him next. Tell him we all miss him."

"Okay, I will."

Halle scanned the hall for someone to run up and check on Wyatt's whereabouts. Nigel, a grade 10, played out the balls scattered across the house billiard table in the corner of the big open room where girls were allowed to mingle with the boys.

"Nigel, oh thank God you're here. I need you," Halle said.

"Why? What's going on? Did someone die?"

"No, but I need you to go get Wyatt for me."

"Really?" Nigel asked, lining up his next shot.

"Really!" Halle said, losing her patience.

Nigel lowered his cue to the table, taking his time to make sure he would hit his target.

"Now, Nigel!" Halle's hand dashed out, stealing the striped ball before the cue ball could strike.

"Jesus, Halle," Nigel whined. "That was going to be the perfect shot." He mounted the stairs. "You don't have to be such a bitch."

"I heard that!" Halle called after him. Nigel's stride quickened.

Halle paced around the billiard table, worrying her lip as she checked the face of her white Michael Kors watch for the fourth time, before finally hearing Wyatt clunk his way down the stairs.

"What's got your panties in a twist," Wyatt asked, walking into the room.

"My panties are none of your concern," Halle replied curtly, grabbing his wrist. "Come with me."

Wyatt resisted for a moment, but then gave in to his curiosity, following her out of the house and around the back to the bench under the western eve of the dormitory. "So give, Halle. Why all the drama?"

"Look!" Halle unclenched her left hand, showing the crumpled wax paper bag held within.

"At a sandwich bag?"

"Not just a bag." Halle couldn't believe he didn't see it.

"Okay?"

"Wyatt, it's a wax paper bag!"

"So? My mum used to wrap crap in them when I was little. What's the big deal?"

"Have you ever seen one since? Like on campus?"

"No, they're stupid. As I remember, they always leaked. You can never keep the damn things closed."

"Exactly!"

"What are you saying?"

"That no one uses these bags anymore; they're obsolete."

"Yeah, so?"

"The person who put the pot in Alex's book bag wrapped it in a wax paper bag. He told me. He said he didn't even know you could buy things like that anymore."

Wyatt took the bag from her hand, smoothing the coated paper between his fingers. "Where did you find this?"

"In the school kitchen. I went in to grab plastic sandwich bags for Mrs. Middleton, and there was a box of them in the same bin."

Wyatt's angular jaw twitched. "You think someone in the kitchen put the pot in Alex's book bag?"

"Yes!"

"I'm not connecting the dots, Halle. You need to help me on this one. Why would anyone in the kitchen want to get Alex booted out of school?"

Halle told Wyatt about what Alex saw on the ferry when they returned after break. Then about what she'd found on the Internet regarding Ramon Perez and Nico Soto.

"I didn't put everything together till I found this bag and remembered Ramon's wife, Lola, had been cleaning tables next to us the morning Alex told us about seeing this Nico guy get killed. She must have overheard us. Her earbuds were in, I know they were, because she was dancing, badly, like really America's-Got-Talent-four-Xs badly, but she had to have heard us. It's the only thing that makes sense."

Halle stood and turned. "It's brilliant, actually. If Alex really did witness a murder, getting kicked out of school would be the perfect way to get him off campus and away from here without anyone asking questions."

"But you said your Mr. Rivero, or Perez, was dealing coke, not pot. They're two completely different drugs."

Halle's face contorted with rage. "I know that. I'm not stupid. But if he's hiding slash selling a massive load of cocaine, what does it matter if he dabbles in a little pot? Remember what they said in planning class in grade ten? Marijuana is the gateway drug," Halle said, finger-quoting the last sentence.

"I wasn't here in grade ten," Wyatt grumbled.

"Whatever, that doesn't matter. I bet Mr. Rivero, or whatever we want to call him, is supplying half the kids on campus with drugs."

"That's a pretty big assumption to make from a wax paper bag."

Halle started to pace the length of the bench where Wyatt sat. "I don't think so. Look up what I've told you online; I'll even send you the links. Think about it, Wyatt: If we can prove that the Riveros are responsible for planting the pot in Alex's bag, Mr. Davies will have to let him back on campus. You'll get your roommate back. I'll get my boyfriend. He'll get to graduate with us. Then his future won't be totally screwed. Wyatt, we can make this right, I know we can."

Wyatt's head began to spin. He cradled his chin on his thumbs and started rubbing circles on his temples with his index fingers. "Okay, let me get this straight. Alex witnessed this guy Nico getting shot on the ferry. Lola, Mr. Rivero's wife—our school cook who can't cook worth shit, I'll give you that—overheard Alex say he witnessed the murder. After hearing what Alex said, Lola planted weed in his backpack to get him kicked out of school. Sound good so far?"

"Yes." Halle nodded, stopping in front of Wyatt.

"But, if that's the case, then why did Lola only get rid of Alex. Why not everyone else sitting at the table that morning?"

"Because," Halle said, deflating. "Izzy and I didn't believe him. We actually laughed when he accused Mr. Rivero of killing someone."

Wyatt leaned forward, shaking his head.

"Alex was right, Wyatt, and I laughed in his face. I suck!"

"Man, this is completely screwed."

"Please, will you help me?"

"Jesus, Halle, if what you're saying is true, these guys are serious drug dealers. Alex is lucky he only got kicked out."

Wyatt stood and rubbed his palms down the front of his black skinny jeans. His straight blond hair hung in front of his eyes, preventing Halle from searching his face for a sign of what he might be thinking.

"Wyatt . . ."

Wyatt held his hand up. "Let me look into a couple things."

"So you'll help?"

"I don't know. I may have an idea, though. Give me a couple days. Until then, watch your ass. If the Riveros think you know something, you'll end up like Alex. Or maybe worse. Don't you have an uncle who's a cop or something? Maybe you should think about giving him a call."

"Thank you!" Halle wrapped her arms around Wyatt's shoulders, hugging him.

Taken off guard, Wyatt tensed against the pressure of her body.

"Alex is right. You're not such a bad guy after all."

CHAPTER 38

"You left this," Mrs. Middleton said, entering Halle's bedroom. In her outstretched hand was Halle's red Herschel pack.

Halle rubbed the back of her neck, feeling the beginning of a headache creep into the side of her skull. "Oops, sorry, Mrs. M."

"Where did you run off to? Is everything okay?"

Halle didn't know how to answer. The only thing that came to mind was the one excuse Missy constantly used whenever she didn't want to do something. "Yeah, everything's fine. I just headed back to the House early because I have cramps, bad ones." Halle winced as she spoke the words, hating the lie.

"Well, see if you can borrow some Midol from one of the other girls if you don't have any yourself."

"I did, thanks."

"Do you think you can finish the job sometime this week?"

"Sure. Can I be excused from dinner tonight, though? I feel like I'm going to throw up." Halle was officially going to hell now. The taste of the fib in her mouth made her tongue swell, and for a second she thought she might actually puke. But she didn't want to run into the Riveros at dinner, no matter what the lie cost her conscience.

"All right, dear."

As soon as the door closed, Halle covered her head with her pillow and screamed into the feathers. She didn't want to call Uncle Mike. She would rather have her wisdom teeth pulled than call, but she knew both Alex and Wyatt were right when they said she should tell him what she found online. Something in her gut told her she was on the right track about this. Maybe her uncle would actually listen to her, even though it all sounded farfetched, at the very least. If he told her to stay out of things, though, Halle already knew she wouldn't listen. Not if she could bring Alex back to campus.

Halle picked up her phone and dialed her uncle's number.

"Uncle Mike?"

"Hey, Hal, not really a good time to chat."

"But I really need to talk to you."

"Okay, Kiddo, but keep it short. I got a lot going on." Halle could already hear the tension in her uncle's voice.

"I want you to check out Ramon Rivero, our school cook. Alex thinks he's the man he saw on the ferry, but I think the guy also might be involved with a cocaine bust in Florida. In fact, I think he might even be Ramon Perez, the dead guy's partner. Look up Nico Soto. I found these old pictures of them online last night."

"Hold on there, Hal." Halle heard her uncle get up and close the door to his office. "What exactly are you talking about and how the hell do you know anything about Nico Soto?"

"The *Times Colonist* had an article about him. Alex saw it and recognized him from the ferry and texted me. I guess I got a little carried away with my online search after I typed in his name and saw what was written."

"Jesus Christ." Uncle Mike exhaled loudly. "Halle, you know I can't talk about an ongoing investigation with you."

"Yeah, but you could have at least informed me that something *did* happen on the ferry we were on—you know, to put Alex's mind at ease. And what about the abandoned car? Couldn't you have mentioned something about that?"

"No, actually, Hal, I couldn't. You told me Alex thought he saw someone getting killed, not that he saw a missing drug dealer. I can't tell you anything more about the car because we haven't found the driver. I have people checking on every angle of this case, Halle. You need to trust me when I tell you that I'm doing my job."

Halle heard her uncle's name being called over the intercom in the background.

"Uncle Mike, there is one more thing."

"Halle, I really need to get going."

"Okay, then I'll be quick. Earlier today I found a wax paper bag when I was in the kitchen running an errand for Mrs. Middleton, just like the one full of pot they found in Alex's pack. No one uses bags like that anymore. I haven't seen one since Mom went on one of her save the environment kicks back in second grade. So let's say Alex really did see the school cook, the guy I think is Ramon Perez, kill this Nico guy. He wouldn't want any witnesses, right? Alex is a witness, and the easiest way to get rid of Alex would be to get him kicked out of school. What's the easiest way to get kicked out? Drugs. See where I'm going with this?"

"Whoa, Hal. This is way out there, even for you. I need more evidence than a wax paper bag and a couple of old Internet pictures. Let's take this one step at a time. Right now I need to find Nico."

"Okay then, what if I could prove our school cook is from Florida? Would you take me more seriously then?"

"Halle!" Halle could hear the irritation in her uncle's voice. It oozed through the phone, sending a chill down her spine. "You are going to let this thing with the Riveros go, do you hear me?"

"Uncle Mike," Halle pleaded. "Can you please just take a look? Google Ramon Perez and then Google Ramon Rivero. Then tell me if I'm crazy."

"Halle, I've got people looking into everything right now. Let us handle this."

CHAPTER 39

Wyatt chewed on the eraser at the end of his mechanical pencil as he reexamined the Internet images on the screen in front of him for the hundredth time, irritated to no end that he agreed with Halle's conclusion.

Scratching his chin, Wyatt thought about the connection between the pot and the Riveros. He wanted confirmation that the drugs had actually come from them before he and Halle did something stupid, like getting involved. He knew how to get weed if he wanted to. Every guy on campus did. God, he wished his dad were still alive. Wyatt could have asked him for advice. He would have known what to do.

Wyatt opened his door and walked down the hall to Jasper Chang's room.

Jasper ran a tight little business on campus: booze, pot, nothing hard, though, no heroin or coke. And he only brought in small quantities. Wyatt also knew he bought his stuff from someone who lived off campus but within walking distance, because Jasper was never seen getting into a cab alone, and he wasn't stupid enough to bring anyone with him when he went on a buying run.

"Hey, man," Jasper said, tipping his chin. His thin, painfully straight black hair stood on end, spiking in a manner that made Wyatt think of some kind of messed-up forest animal. Jasper's eyes didn't leave his computer screen.

"Dude, can we talk?"

"Sure," Jasper said, shutting his laptop.

Wyatt checked for Jasper's roommate but they were alone, so he shut the door, ensuring they wouldn't be overheard.

"I'm stressed to the tits. You got any pot I can buy?"

"No, man, I'm all out. But I'm buying soon. How much you want?"

"A half ounce or so. But BC bud; I want local."

"Hey, man, I only got what I got."

"Who do you buy from?"

Jasper frowned. "Dude, you know the code. Never reveal your source."

"I know, but I heard the stuff you got last time was bad, gave a lot of people headaches. I don't want that."

"Screw you, Wyatt. Who are you to get all picky about shit?"

"Whatever, man, I'm just telling you what I want."

"Fine. I'm meeting with my source on Friday. If you want in, get me money by tomorrow night."

CHAPTER 40

Sweat trickled down Halle's neck. She wiped it with a towel then bumped up the resistance on her treadmill, hoping to outrun her problems. The rain kept her from running outside, where she preferred, but she missed practice yesterday, and if she didn't do something her coach might scratch her from the next regatta.

She hadn't talked to Wyatt since dragging him out of the house yesterday. She tried approaching him after class, but he'd disappeared before she could open her mouth. Ignoring her completely. He probably thought she lost her mind or something. He wouldn't be the first. Halle rarely filtered what came out of her mouth. Not that she really cared what Wyatt thought, but she really needed his help, for Alex's sake.

"Missy was all over Wyatt in second period again," Izzy gossiped from the machine next to hers.

Halle thought about telling Izzy what she found in the kitchen but knew she would go straight to Alex, and Halle didn't want that to happen yet. Halle shook her head. "Honestly? What do girls see in him?"

"I don't know. I guess he's kind of cute."

"Ew."

"Hey, some people like pretty boys."

"Iz, he wears skinny jeans that are tighter than mine. That's a bit beyond the whole pretty thing; that's boy band wannabe."

Izzy laughed, jumping onto the rails of her treadmill. She grabbed her water bottle. "You know," she said, taking a quick sip, "his tight pants might be the reason he acts like such a jerk. Can you imagine what pants like his do to a guy's junk?"

Halle gagged. "Okay, seriously? Thinking about what goes on in Wyatt's pants is like the last thing I want to think about. Especially while I'm trying to run."

"Whatever." Izzy waved her fingers and slowed her treadmill to a stop. "I'm going to lift some weights."

"Sure you are," Halle smirked, spotting Jacob's slender frame entering the building. "Iz?"

"Yeah?"

"I'm happy for you and Jacob. I really am. I'm sorry I haven't wanted to hang out. It's just still a little hard for me, that's all."

Izzy nodded. "I know, but thanks for saying something."

Halle fumbled with her iPhone, queuing up a playlist as soon as her earbuds were in place. AC/DC's "Thunderstruck" blared through the mini speaker. "There," she sighed, setting her pace to sync with the beat of the classic rock tune. Joan Jett's "I love Rock N' Roll" followed. Screw the top forty, she thought. This music is so much better sometimes.

A fist banged on the window in front of her machine, making Halle leap onto the rails of the treadmill, her hand clutching her chest. On the other side of the pane, Wyatt laughed, his shoulders rising and falling at her expense. Reflexively, her middle finger extended.

Come here, Wyatt mouthed, motioning for her to join him.

Halle turned toward Katie, a grade 10 now running in Izzy's old spot. "Watch this, will you?" Halle asked, leaving her phone and water bottle in the tray by the controls so someone else wouldn't take over the machine.

Katie nodded.

"Thanks, I'll be right back."

Grassy puddles surrounded the cement walkways approaching the gym. Halle noticed goose bumps on her arms as she stepped out into the cold, damp air. "What?"

"Hi to you too," Wyatt sneered. His black all-weather coat zipped to his chin made Halle wish she'd grabbed her sweatshirt before heading out to meet him. He looked warm.

Halle waved her hand in the air. "Whatever. I thought we established a truce yesterday. Then again, I thought you'd talk to me this morning after class, so what do I know."

"Is that what you're pissed about, me not saying hi to you in a classroom? Needy much? I told you I had to figure a couple things out first, that's all. Man, you have some serious princess issues if you're mad about that."

"I do not have princess issues." Halle clenched her teeth, shivering.

"You're cold."

"Ah, yeah. It's kind of freezing out here."

"Why didn't you grab a coat?"

Halle shrugged. "I thought I'd be right back in. Now, are you going to finally tell me why you're here?"

Wyatt unzipped his coat and placed it over Halle's shoulders.

"Th-th-thanks," she stuttered, slightly shocked by his kindness.

Wyatt scanned the front of the gym to make sure no one could hear what he had to say before speaking. "I started thinking about something you said, about how you thought Mr. Rivero might sell drugs to the students. I want to see if that's true. So I asked Jasper Chang, the grade eleven in my house, if he could get me some pot. He's the go-to guy for this sort of thing."

Halle's eyes widened. "Really?"

"He said he didn't have any, but he's going on a buy run in a couple days. If I give him some cash, he can get me something, which, for your information, is what I was doing this morning. Do you have unsupervised prep tonight? Can you meet me at the student center around eight thirty?"

"Yeah."

"We'll talk then." Wyatt stepped back.

"Wait, your coat."

"You got something you can use after your run in there?"

"Yeah, I've got my rowing hoodie back inside, in a cubby." Halle slipped off the coat and handed it to the stranger in front of her. "Thanks."

She didn't know this Wyatt. He could almost be called nice, offering his coat to her like that.

Wyatt shook his head, sensing Halle's unease. "Chill, Halle. I just offered you my coat so you wouldn't catch a cold before Alex comes back to school. He would probably blame me if you got sick and he knew we were hanging out. I seem to be the first to come to peoples' minds."

Halle rolled her eyes. "See you tonight."

"Sounds good."

CHAPTER 41

Izzy sat on her bed twirling her pen in the air, thinking about what she wanted to write next. "Ahhh . . . I hate homework!"

"Tell me about it." Halle looked back down at the open books on her desk, wrapping the loose hair hanging in her face around her finger.

"Are you going out tonight?" asked Izzy.

"Yeah, I think so. Wyatt wanted to meet up."

"Wow, that's new. You guys getting along better after you apologized to him the other day?"

"Yeah, I'm trying. I think it will make Alex happy if he knows we're not fighting anymore."

"Probably. Alex might even be jealous that you two are meeting up if you didn't look like that."

"What do you mean?" Halle said. "I rock this look." Halle's red sweatshirt, littered with bleach stains, was zipped over the torn hem of the vintage Pink Floyd concert T-shirt she stole from her dad years ago. Her faded yoga capris looked more gray than black from so many washes.

"You're just jealous."

Izzy laughed. "You caught me."

"How about you. Are you going out?"

"No. Jacob left for Vancouver after dinner with the tennis team. I thought I'd watch a movie. If you're going to the student center, though, will you bring me back a strawberry smoothie?"

Halle slipped the hairband from her wrist and wrapped her hair into a messy bun. "Sure. I'm getting some sweet potato fries, too. What do you think you're going to watch? I'll bring you food if you promise we can watch one of the *Transformer* movies."

"Deal."

Halle smiled and headed toward the door. She slid her feet into her UGGs then pulled her electric blue Marc Jacobs purse over her head, her favorite designer; she had one of his leather coats, too, but rarely wore such nice things on campus. Her current outfit was pretty atrocious, but what did she care? She certainly didn't feel like she needed to impress anyone, least of all Wyatt.

CHAPTER 42

Wyatt sat by himself at a booth in the middle of the room. Halle could see only the back of his head, his always-perfect white-blond hair styled with an abundance of product.

"Hey," Halle said, walking up to him.

"Hey." Wyatt sat drumming his fingers across the wood-trimmed Formica tabletop.

Halle slid into the booth across from him. "So?"

"Jasper's going to his supplier on Friday. All I know is that he buys somewhere close to campus. I thought we'd follow him, see where he goes, if it is Rivero he buys from and if the stuff is wrapped in those stupid waxed bags you found in the kitchen.

Halle nodded. "Then, depending on what we find out, we can figure out how to proceed from there, right?"

"Yeah, but let's not jump ahead of ourselves. First, we have to link the pot to the big guy in the kitchen. I looked at the pictures you told me about online. They're really grainy. I couldn't tell you if it's our cook or not, nor will anyone else. But, yeah I agree. It seems worth looking into."

Halle heard her phone buzz on the cushion next to her. *Don't forget ketchup*, her roommate's text reminded her.

"Stay here, don't go anywhere," Halle warned, rising. "I have to put in a food order. Do you want anything?"

Wyatt shook his head as Halle scooted from the booth and headed toward the food service counter at the far side of the room.

Returning, Halle saw Missy standing beside Wyatt at their table. Their hushed conversation looked heated. She wished she could hear what he was saying. Missy threw her arms into the air as her foot tapped insistently.

"Hey," Halle said to Missy, sliding back into her spot.

Missy sucked in a breath, holding it for several seconds. "So is this who you're with now? The reason why you won't let me sit down and don't want to hang out anymore, Wyatt?"

"Chill, Missy. Halle and I are just talking. I don't want to hang out with you anymore because I'm sick of all the drama you create. When you're not attacking my face you're telling everyone I'm partying it up at school when I'm not. I don't want trouble just because you need something to talk about."

Leering, Missy turned her venomous attention on Halle. "Cheating on Alex with his roommate? That's tacky, even for you, Halle."

Halle watched tiny droplets of spit fly from Missy's mouth as she talked. Squeezing the ketchup packets in her hand, Halle wished that one of them would break, spraying Missy's overly made-up face in sweet, sticky tomato sauce.

"Wyatt and I are friends, Missy. I'm still with Alex."

"Ha," Missy said, tipping her chin up.

"Friends?" Wyatt repeated, his brow rising.

"Yeah," Halle confirmed. "You loaned me your coat this afternoon. I think that's a step in the right direction. Besides, Alex always said we'd get along if we gave each other a chance."

Wyatt didn't have many friends. He liked the sound of it rolling off Halle's tongue.

"Isn't that sweet," Missy hissed. "I'll bet Alex will be interested to hear about how cozy you two—"

"Shut up, Missy," said Wyatt, interrupting her with a wave of his hand.

"You can't tell me to shut up," Missy said, snapping her fingers in his face.

"The hell I can't. You're way off base."

Missy stamped her foot. "Really? 'Cause I'm just telling what it looks like."

Wyatt shook his head. "Halle, you want to hook up with me?"

Halle cringed. "Uh, no."

"Good, then no offence but you're the last person on campus I want to get with either."

Missy scowled.

"So, now that that's settled, are you done harassing Halle?" Wyatt asked, already bored with Missy's self-induced drama.

Missy looked from Halle to Wyatt. "Excuse me?" she said, placing her hands on her hips.

"You heard me. If you're done making up these bullshit stories about Halle and me getting together then it's time for you to leave. She and I have things to discuss which don't involve you."

Missy gasped. "We are over, Wyatt Donley! You hear me? *O-V-E-R* over!"

"Fine with me."

Missy screamed in frustration and stormed away from the table.

Halle steepled her fingers. "Well, that was interesting."

"You're telling me." A couple of groups milling around the other tables were staring at them.

"Guess we just gave the rumor mill something new to talk about," Halle said.

"Do you care?" Wyatt asked tentatively.

"Not if you don't."

"Good," said Wyatt, feeling pleasantly surprised.

"Any other jealous freaks I should know about? Now would be a good time to tell me."

Wyatt chuckled. "Nope. Missy was fun while she lasted, but that chick has some serious anger-management issues."

"You're telling me."

Turning serious, Wyatt added, "Besides, I don't let anyone put my friends down."

Halle grinned, happy that she and Wyatt seemed to be on the same page for once. "Good, me neither."

Wyatt yawned and stretched his arms in front of him. "Now, where were we?"

"About to discuss how to follow Jasper."

"Right, here's the deal. If Jasper doesn't meet up with one of the Riveros on Friday night but still brings me a wax paper bag full of shit, you have to promise me you'll leave this thing with them alone. If he gets it from some random dude, we need to leave this murder thing with the Riveros to the police. Understand? Let the cops bust them if it's not going to bring Alex back. I did some research myself. If Mr. Rivero's the guy we think he is, he's a dangerous SOB. If he thinks you're on to him, there's no telling what he'll do. The risk isn't worth putting yourself in that position. As it is, you and Izzy, and whoever else was at that table, need to watch your ass."

Humor lit Halle's eyes. "Aw, does that mean you really care about me?"

Wyatt rolled his eyes. "God, you're annoying. I care about my roommate. The jury's still out on you."

"Hey, I thought we were officially friends now."

"I'm serious, Halle."

"All right." Halle sighed, giving up. "I promise."

"Good, then here's how it's going to go."

CHAPTER 43

"The only thing I haven't figured out is what we're going to do if Jasper sees us following him. He'll be pissed if he sees me, but I wouldn't stop him from doing the buy. If he sees you, though, he'll know something's up, and the deal will be off." Wyatt ran his hand through his hair, messing the gel up slightly before straightening the pieces once again. "Maybe I should go by myself."

"No," Halle said flatly.

"I don't know. Is getting discovered really worth the risk?"

"We won't get discovered."

"How can you say that?"

"Promise you won't make fun of me?"

Wyatt tapped his chin with his forefinger. "I don't know; with our history, can I really promise you anything?"

Halle glared at him, exhaling loudly. "Seriously?"

"Okay, okay," Wyatt chuckled, raising his hands in the air. "I won't tease you."

"I have a way we can follow him without getting spotted." Reaching into her purse, Halle pulled out the spy purchases she'd made the week before.

"What the hell is this?"

"Well . . ." Halle sighed.

"A GPS tracker? Infrared night vision goggles? Halle, you want to tell me where all this came from?"

"The Internet. But if we're being honest with each other now, I should probably mention that I bought all of this when I thought you were behind Alex getting kicked out."

Wyatt's eyes grew wide. "What exactly were you going to do to me?"

Halle shrugged. "I don't know. Prove Alex's innocence? I didn't exactly think before I acted."

Wyatt fingered the tiny tracker. "Man, I didn't think they really made this stuff for the general public. I mean, I had toys like this when I was little, but . . . Did you get this from Amazon?"

"Actually, I ordered it from the Spy Shop on Amazon."

"Ha, really?"

Halle nodded. "I kind of tend to overdo things when I'm pissed."

"You think?"

Halle's nose wrinkled. "Hey, I've already said I was sorry, twice. Don't make me do it a third time."

"Man, remind me not to set you off again."

"Yeah, probably not a good idea."

Wyatt laughed. "Damn, Halle."

"I want Alex back with us, Wyatt. He doesn't deserve what happened to him."

"I know. I totally agree. Why do you think I'm doing this?"

From behind the food service counter, a man with a hair net yelled, "Order for Henry, you're up."

"That's me," Halle said. "Thanks, Wyatt, for everything."

Wyatt's flawless face eased into a smile. "See you tomorrow."

CHAPTER 44

Halle took her time walking back up the hill to her dorm. Her first opinions of people were usually spot-on. With Wyatt, though, she'd been wrong and glad of it. She dipped her hand into the white, grease-stained sack containing the french fries, pulling one out. The clouds overhead parted. For the first time in days, Halle could see stars in the sky. A massive waxing moon illuminated the path. When she finished the fry she licked the salt from her fingers.

In front of her, she could see the lit-up backgrounds of her friends' rooms in Campbell House, to her side, the rooms of Alex's old dormitory. She grabbed a second fry, cursing the greasy potato's addictive flavor. "We're bringing you back, Alex," she said, raising the fry toward the window that used to be his. "I promised you we'd be together again, and I never break a promise."

•

April 14, 2015 10:20 PM

Halle: Hey.

      Alex: Hey.

Halle: I think I made peace with your roommate.

      Alex: Oh yeah?

Halle: We met up earlier tonight. Actually talked some stuff out. Decided we made better friends than enemies. You proud of me or what?

      Alex: Totally.

Halle: I know right :)

      Alex: What did you talk about?

Halle: You & how we both wish you were here.

      Alex: I know. I miss you guys too.

Halle: I hate fighting with you.

>**Alex:** Me too. I've just been so stressed out recently. It's crazy.

Halle: Me too.

>**Alex:** I think I talked my parents into letting you come home with Iz next break so I can see you. Things are going better. I got waitlisted at USC.

Halle: That's great! They're totally going to let you in.

>**Alex:** Yeah the admissions guy said I have to keep my grades up & they'll let me know by the end of the month.

Halle: It will happen don't worry :)

>**Alex:** Anything else going on?

Halle: Just watched Transformers 3 with your sister.

>**Alex:** I love that movie!

Halle: I know right? Totally the best one they've made.

>**Alex:** I don't know. I like the 2nd one. Megan Fox is hot.

Halle: Oh…I should probably warn you. Missy is telling everyone Wyatt & I are hooking up. She saw us together tonight & freaked. He told her to shut up & dumped her in front of everyone at the Ritz. Priceless!

>**Alex:** No way. That's hysterical. Thanks for the warning, but no one's going to believe her. They all know you're still crazy about me. ;)

Halle: I don't know. People are stupid. I might not mind Wyatt anymore, but the thought of kissing him still makes me ill. Now the new spring exchange from New Zealand…

>**Alex:** Umm…Boyfriend here.

Halle: :) jk

>**Alex:** You're killing me!

Halle: I'm trying to <3

        Alex: Brat!

Halle: :p

CHAPTER 45

Wyatt clutched the GPS tracker in the front pocket of his pants. The thing was no bigger than his mum's BMW key, but square with rounded corners, lighter too. He already linked the device to his and Halle's cell phones. When one of them pulled up the coordinating app the tracker turned on, locating the wearer's position. Wild technology.

"Halle," Wyatt mumbled to the empty hall, shaking his head, a goofy grin parting his lips. She'd definitely grown on him. If he had a sister, he imagined the relationship would be similar. He felt oddly protective over her now that they were spending so much time together. She didn't care what people said about them either, a refreshing change of attitude compared to most of the females he knew. He still couldn't get over how many times he had already heard girls in his classes casually calling Halle a slut just because they were now friends. People loved to jump to the wrong conclusions. He flipped the tracker around in the palm of his hand. Now he just needed to hide the thing so that Jasper wouldn't notice he was carrying it.

During classes, Lockhart House stood virtually empty. Mrs. Scott and the little girls might be in residence, and maybe another grade 12 or two, but that was all. Mr. Scott would be coaching up at the rugby pitch, their season in full swing now. The glory of being in your last year at Lakeview was that the school allowed you one spare class to do with as you pleased. If you had the credits, you could choose nothing, which he did. Occasionally, he slept; more often than not he played video games. The clanking of someone messing around on the second floor echoed through the stairwell.

Wyatt stood outside Jasper's door. He could hear the *tick, tick, tick* of the second hand on the wall clock. Time seemed to slow down.

Breaking into someone's place felt off, wrong even. He intended to leave something, though, not take. Did that make breaking into his room any better? *Tick*. He slowly pushed open the door.

"Anyone here?" Wyatt asked, knowing the answer. His mouth felt dry, his tongue sticking to the roof of it.

Earlier in the week they decided on placing the tracker in Jasper's coat, a navy-blue zip-up he liked, the weather still not warm enough to go out without something. Halle came up with the idea. Wyatt never noticed what guys wore; girls, maybe, if the clothing clung a little too tightly or dipped lower than the school dress code allowed, but a guy, never. The jacket made sense, though, since they didn't know if he would take a pack. He checked the back of Jasper's chair first.

The chair was empty. Wyatt groaned and moved to the closet. Jasper's dirty clothes lay in piles on the floor: socks, T-shirts, underwear. The dude wore tighty-whiteys, seriously? No one wore nut huggers any more. Pathetic. The odor was overwhelming. *Thunk*. Someone in the rooms above moved a chair. Where the hell was the coat? *Tick*.

Wyatt pawed through the hangers before finally spotting the jacket swinging from a hook mounted on the inside of the door. He opened the coat, checking the pockets: a crushed half-packet of Marlboro Reds, gum, an empty container of Altoids. A rip in the lining on the right-hand side left a gap between the fleece and the waterproof backing, just big enough for the tracker. He pinned it in. Halle made him bring the large safety pin. At the time, he laughed at her for being ridiculous, but now, humbled, he needed to admit the idea had been a good one. He patted the place where he'd pinned the tracker, making sure the device was secured and would go unnoticed. *Tick*. Wyatt closed the closet door and moved back into the hall, taking his first full breath since entering Jasper's room.

CHAPTER 46

The buzz of voices echoing throughout Mason Hall seemed louder than usual. Then again, Fridays were like that.

"Are you playing ping pong tomorrow?" Izzy asked Halle.

"Not if I can help it. You signed me up for dodgeball tonight, anyway, remember?"

The houses competed against each other throughout the year with four different rotations: track and field, soccer, court sports, and indoor games, the latter being Halle's least favorite, which happened to be the next in line.

Izzy playfully stuck her tongue out at Halle. "Yeah, I remember. Do you know who we play first?"

"Kelly, I think."

Campbell House led the game count for wins so far this year. If they kept it up they would take the House Cup for the first time since her good friend Leigh graduated, four years ago.

Halle pushed the remainder of her chicken salad wrap around her plate, questioning the digestibility of the tortilla. Something red and plastic looking appeared between chunks of what they were told was chicken but tasted more like rubber. "I am not eating this." Three more classes, tutorial, then sport, after which she could fix herself a box of Kraft Dinner back in her dorm. Halle thought she might even have a bell pepper or two in the mini refrigerator they kept in the corner of their room.

Izzy got up from the table and picked up her nearly full plate. "I'm done. You coming?"

"Yeah."

Jacob waited for them next to the piles of nondescript backpacks on the entry level of the dining hall.

"Be right there," Halle said, unzipping hers.

"Okay, but hurry. I can't get another tardy if we're late to class or I'll be gated. I do not want to have to stay in the dorm after study hall for the rest of the week."

Halle nodded. "I'll meet you there." She peered into the half-empty canvas pack, moving her books to one side, then the other. She promised Wyatt she would check her pack every time she left the thing unattended.

As she bent over, she pulled down the back of her kilt so that she didn't flash anyone passing behind her. No one needed to see her underwear. Looking around, she wished more girls pulled down their kilts, too. What was wrong with girls these days? A piece of hair fell into her face, and she pushed the offending lock behind her ear.

Unlike Alex's cool leather satchel, Halle's bright red Herschel pack seemed boring. Her mom bought it for her at the beginning of her grade 11 year. The fabric was just beginning to tear around the top of the strap, but she knew she could make the thing work a little longer. Not that it would cost that much to replace, but she'd rather spend her money on the new Elizabeth Roberts purse she had her eye on than a boring old backpack. The designer's new spring line looked amazing. Halle couldn't wait to have enough money saved to buy the piece she wanted. Besides, the purse would look way cuter on a college campus than a canvas pack. After all, only a few months of high school remained. She had received her letter of acceptance to the University of Saint Andrews last week but was still waiting to hear from Oxford, her first choice.

"Hey," said Wyatt, knocking her with his leg as he passed.

Halle flinched as her fingers brushed something foreign in the bag's interior pencil pouch. Plastic, smooth, and . . . Halle looked up at Wyatt, her eyes wide in panic.

"What?"

"I don't know."

Wyatt's eyes followed Halle's arm into the main compartment of her bag.

"Come here." He jerked her hand away, zipped up the pack, threw it over his shoulder, and pulled Halle to her feet, then led her quickly down the hall toward the washrooms.

There were two bathrooms on this level of the building, single stalls with locking doors. Wyatt knocked on the first one. When no one answered, he pushed Halle inside and locked the door behind them. "Open your bag."

"It's in the pencil pouch."

Wyatt pulled out a small plastic bag full of white powder. "Shit, Hal. Goddamnit. This is bad!" Wyatt struck the paper towel holder with the palm of his hand.

"Is that what I think it is?"

"Yeah."

"Cocaine?" Halle squeaked, still unsure.

Wyatt held the bag of white powder over the toilet.

"What are you doing?"

"What does it look like? I'm getting rid of it."

Halle started shaking. "But you can't flush a plastic bag."

"Watch me."

Wyatt emptied the contents directly into the water, flushed, wiped down the rim, rinsed out the baggie, and then flushed again. The third time, he ripped the bag into shreds and watched the plastic disappear in a swirl of water before soaping his hands.

"There," he said, swabbing down the counter with a moistened towel. Halle stared into the empty toilet bowl. Wyatt snapped his fingers in front of her face. "Earth to Halle. You okay?"

Halle nodded, unable to speak.

Wyatt pawed through the rest of her things, just to make sure nothing else remained.

CHAPTER 47

Wyatt held the door to the bathroom open for Halle, letting her walk through before him. Her body swayed. The smile plastered on her face was definitely fake. "Do you get how dangerous this whole situation is for you now?" he said, placing his hand on Halle's back to steady her. "I got a hundie on the fact that you'll get called into Mr. Davies's office before the end of next period, so you need to pull yourself together."

Halle looked up, her eyes locking onto his, piercing hazel orbs anchored by large black pupils. "I know."

"We should end this."

"No."

"Coke isn't like pot, Halle. If you're caught with something this hardcore on your person you're expelled and most likely arrested immediately when the authorities get called in. Which I'm sure they do with something this serious. You can kiss your college acceptance letters goodbye. Your future is over."

"That's exactly why we can't stop, Wyatt. Next time they'll go after Izzy, then Jacob. Now that we're hanging out they might even go after you. No, we have to figure out who's behind this and stop them, before anyone else's life is ruined."

They walked down the hall, exiting the building together. The cherry trees in the main quad were just starting to bloom, filling the grassy corridor with pink blossoms.

Wyatt was adamant. "Damn it, Halle, are you even listening to yourself?"

Halle stopped walking.

He shoved his hands into the front pocket of his gray flannel pants. "How the hell does Alex even put up with you?"

Halle's shoulders sagged. "Can we maybe not mention any of this to him? He got pretty pissed the last time I brought up the whole thing with the Riveros."

"You think?" Wyatt said, shaking his head. "The guy's crazy about you, Halle. He'd rip my frickin' head off if he knew what we were up to."

"So you'll still help me?"

"Well, I'm not going to let you try and take on the Riveros by yourself. Which, by the way, I know you'll do if I don't help you."

Halle nodded. "Thank you."

Wyatt slowly shook his head. "You're impossible, you know that?"

"Yeah, I've heard that before."

CHAPTER 48

"I saw you after lunch with Wyatt," Missy said. "You make me sick."

Halle wanted to scream. This so wasn't her day.

"Shut up, Missy," Izzy said, overhearing Missy and stepping up to stand by her friend.

"She's cheating on your brother and you're telling me to shut up?"

"Yeah, because they're just friends, and you're telling everyone lies about them hooking up because he's not into you anymore."

The venom in Izzy's voice as she defended her made Halle want to leap over and hug her roommate.

Missy flipped her hair and stormed ahead of them to her desk.

"Did you just tell Missy off for me?"

Izzy straightened her back. "Yeah."

"Holy crap, Iz, I'm so proud of you."

"Well, don't be. She had it coming. I swear, if I hear one more lie about you, Alex, or Wyatt come out of her mouth I'm going to puke."

Halle grinned. "I'm wearing off on you, aren't I? Pretty soon you're going to be saying whatever comes to mind, out loud, just like me."

"Maybe, maybe not, don't get your hopes up. I'm just sick of all the gossip. It's not healthy for any of us."

"You're right," Halle agreed.

"Now, would you care to tell me what Missy meant by saying she saw you with Wyatt after lunch?"

Halle knew she needed to fill Izzy in on everything she and Wyatt were doing. Just not here, in front of their classmates.

Izzy searched her friend's worried face. "Is everything all right?"

A knock sounded on the door. Mrs. Sloan, the office assistant, stood in the frame. "Miss Henry, will you please follow me."

Taking a deep breath, she collected her things.

"What's going on?" Izzy whispered.

"I'll tell you when I get back."

•

The sound of Halle's loafers and Mrs. Sloan's heels echoed down the empty hall, Halle's nerves fraying more with each step. The fact that Mrs. Sloan hadn't used her first name when she called her out of the classroom made Halle wary. The woman had been her grade 8 and 9 field hockey coach. Sure, she hadn't been one of the top players, but they'd always gotten along . . . well, as much as anyone could with her. Still, Halle was sure Mrs. Sloan wouldn't have forgotten her name.

"Sit here, please," said Mrs. Sloan when they entered the office.

The thick paneled door to the dean's office opened. "This way, young lady." Mr. Davies ushered her forward. As she passed, he took the strap of her backpack between his thumb and fingertips, as if the fabric contained an infectious disease, and placed it on his desk in front of them.

"I just received a rather distressing anonymous message from a member of our staff," he said, turning to Halle, his hands now clasped behind his back. He stood an inch or two taller than she did; not enough to be considered a tall man, by any means, but at the moment, at least to Halle, he seemed like a giant.

"What about?" Halle asked, trying to hide shaking hands by tucking them under her armpits. She badly wanted to ask Mr. Davies how he knew the message came from a staff member if it was truly anonymous. Halle sucked her lower lip between her teeth, biting hard enough to draw blood, the metallic taste filling her mouth.

"Is there anything you'd like to tell me before we proceed?" Mr. Davies asked.

Halle took the seat he offered in front of his desk.

Mr. Davies sat down and pushed a stack of student papers to the side. "I just got off the phone with Mrs. Middleton. I've asked her to conduct a search of your room as we speak."

"Why?" Halle said, finding her courage, anger replacing fear.

Mr. Davies brought his palms together. "We have reason to believe there are drugs in your possession."

"Excuse me? Shouldn't you test me or something before you start going through my stuff?"

"Are you afraid we might find something in your room?"

"No, it's just I've never been in your office before. I've never been accused of doing anything and I've never even been in trouble with the school before. I've maintained a three-point-six GPA or better every year I've been here, and I would think you'd at least give me the benefit of the doubt before you accuse me of something I didn't do."

Mr. Davies flexed his hands. Halle briefly squeezed her eyes shut, wishing the moment away.

"Will you at least tell me what you're looking for?" Halle asked.

Mr. Davies looked disgusted. "Your flippant attitude will do little for you in your current situation."

Halle's eyes narrowed. "I'm sorry if I'm being short, Mr. Davies. I'm just a bit confused. You just yanked me out of class, provincial testing is next month, and I'd like to get back to my studies. I have never done drugs, and I don't plan on experimenting with them any time soon."

"We shall see."

Not making a sound, Mrs. Sloan appeared in the doorway behind Halle.

"Margaret," Mr. Davies said. "Would you mind helping me?"

Together, Mr. Davies and Mrs. Sloan searched the contents of Halle's bag.

"It's clean," Mrs. Sloan concluded, zipping the pack back up.

Mr. Davies took a deep breath. "Miss Henry, someone said they saw you place a suspicious white powder resembling cocaine into your bag earlier today."

Halle felt like someone was smothering her with a pillow. She took a shallow breath. "Well, I didn't!" She thought of Alex.

The phone on Mr. Davies's desk rang. Raising a finger into the air, he silenced her. Halle could hear Mrs. Middleton's voice come through the receiver.

"I see. Thank you, Eleanor." Mr. Davies hung up. "Miss Henry, Halle, here at Lakeview we take drug-related accusations extremely seriously. Mrs. Middleton just reported that there was nothing in your room and that she has the utmost respect for you. That being said, I am still going to insist that you be tested."

"Of course."

CHAPTER 49

Halle picked up the cup on Mrs. Sloan's desk on her way out and stomped down the hall, container in hand. Thank God it was during class time so no one would see her taking the walk of shame. The gossip whores would go crazy with something like this. Halle shivered just thinking of the false crap people would say just to prop themselves up into a higher social standing. When she finished and the test returned negative, Mr. Davies dismissed her, apologizing for the inconvenience.

"Keep out of trouble, Miss Henry," he said. Which sounded more like "we'll be watching you" to Halle. The plot line for George Orwell's *1984*, a book they just read for English, popped into her mind. She looked up to where the walls met the ceiling, half expecting to see observation cameras mounted in the corners.

Halle tossed her backpack over her shoulder, running her hands down the straps until they reached the red canvas body of the bag. She wanted answers. Hoping Mrs. Middleton would give them to her, she decided to head to the library. A couple of students pushed the heavy glass doors open, heading to other classes.

"I thought I might see you sooner rather than later," her dorm mother said, spotting her.

Halle tossed her things on the floor next to Mrs. Middleton's workstation. "Who told Mr. Davies I was carrying coke, Mrs. M?"

Mrs. Middleton paused. "Does it matter?"

"Yes, it matters! Someone accused me of doing drugs when I'm not. I want to know who."

"I don't know who it was, Halle. I think you know that."

"Why? Why won't you tell me? This is crap."

"It was a staff member. Mr. Davies never said who. It's school policy not to put staff against student."

"Was it the same staff member that told Mr. Davies about Alex having pot in his backpack?"

"Halle, Alex did have marijuana in his backpack. You, thankfully, did not. "

Mrs. Middleton looked like she was trying to decide what to say next.

Halle was confident that if she put money down on the informer being one of the Riveros she'd hit the jackpot.

"Did you ever stop to think that maybe Alex was framed?"

"Halle, I know you. Don't let your imagination run wild. There isn't some kind of conspiracy against Alex. Who in the world would want to frame him! What would the school gain from expelling two of its top students under false pretenses? What happened to Alex was his fault. You both know the school's substance abuse policy. I'm just glad the person who reported you was wrong."

Halle wanted to tell Mrs. Middleton everything. The accusations were perched on the tip of her tongue, longing to be said, but she swallowed them back. She could feel the veins in her forehead pulse as a migraine threatened to make its presence known.

Mrs. Middleton returned her attention to the computer screen sitting on her desk, her rigid posture, tense shoulders, and focused gaze signaling the end to the conversation. "The bell is about to ring, Halle. You'd better get to your next class."

CHAPTER 50

Izzy spotted Halle on the path to the science building. "So what did Mrs. Sloan want? Why did they pull you out of class? Halle, what the hell is going on?" She fired off the rapid questions between breaths, sprinting to catch up with Halle.

Halle took a deep breath. "Mr. Davies accused me of having cocaine in my backpack."

Izzy stopped midstep. "What the hell?"

"Exactly!" Halle's eyes started to fill. She'd held her tears in all morning, not letting her frustrations show, but seeing Izzy brought her emotions back up to the surface.

"Come here," Izzy said, wrapping her arms around her roommate.

Halle could only nod. "It's just all so much," she choked out.

Izzy held Halle until she felt her breathing even out and return to normal. "I got gossip. Would that help take your mind off things?"

Halle wiggled from Izzy's embrace, shaking her head in disbelief. "Iz, I just had to take a drug test for the first time in my life. I'm not really in the mood."

"I know, but I'm trying to distract you so you don't have to think about it. I haven't seen you laugh in days. I want the old Halle back, the one who laughs all the time. You had to piss in a cup, so what, who hasn't."

"Ah, you."

"Sure I have, at the doctor's office when I was sick, duh."

"You were like twelve."

"Thirteen, thank you."

"Well, they didn't test you for illegal substances."

Izzy rolled her eyes. "Yeah, but I still had to pee in a cup. That's what you said."

"You're a dork."

"I know," Izzy said with an easy smile, satisfied she had lightened the mood a bit.

"Thanks, Iz." Halle paused and picked at her peeling lip with her fingers. "We should talk. There's something you should know," she finally said, deciding to tell Izzy everything. For all she knew, the Riveros would go after Izzy next.

"Tell me later," Izzy said, pulling Halle toward their next class. "First, let me tell you what I heard."

CHAPTER 51

Wyatt watched Halle from across their Writing 12 classroom. She sat next to her roommate, Alex's sister—same dark olive skin, smile, and piercing sky-blue eyes. The similarities stopped there, however. Izzy could be nice, but she was loud, almost annoying if you asked him.

Halle's hair seemed messier than her usual I-could-care-less updo. Long strands of brown cascaded down her back, like she'd run her hands through the tangles, forgetting the mess had been tied back. Unconsciously, Wyatt reached up, checking to make sure his hair sat neatly in place.

Wyatt wondered if she'd been called into the office yet. By the look of things, he guessed she had.

He didn't want to care about Halle. But he found it hard not to. Through her sarcastic veneer he saw loyalty, something he didn't see often these days. Something he valued in people more than anything else.

Finding the drugs in her pack earlier scared the crap out of him. It made what they were doing real, very real.

Somewhere in the back of his head, Wyatt thought of the bad '80s movie he'd seen, on a Sunday afternoon at home, about a group of kids getting in trouble with a gang of local drug dealers. The similarities made him cringe.

What if he hadn't seen her on the steps and gone over to say hi after lunch? Would Halle have known what to do? Would she have panicked? All Wyatt knew was that Halle needed him, and, strangely enough, he liked being needed.

Wyatt watched her take out her notebook. Her hands were shaking slightly. Yeah, she'd definitely seen Mr. Davies, he concluded. The man tended to have that effect on people. Wyatt visited his office weekly to perform his mother's so-called "checks," and they'd gotten to know each other relatively well. Mr. Davies came off like a hardass, he needed to for his job, but the guy really wasn't that bad. He loved his wife, had two grown sons, and liked to see the students succeed, that's all. Being in charge of discipline in a school such as Lakeview Academy couldn't be easy. Wyatt felt sorry for the guy—almost.

Halle glanced up at Wyatt and their eyes locked briefly.

He wouldn't let her down. He knew he only promised Alex he would be civil to Halle, but things change.

The teacher started his lecture.

CHAPTER 52

"Why is Wyatt staring at you?" Izzy whispered as the teacher began class.

"I don't know."

Wyatt nodded at Halle, his gaze intense, then turned toward the front of the room after Halle did the same.

"Is this about what happened after lunch? Man, why do I always miss the good stuff? Does he know you had to take a drug test? I am literally dying here," Izzy moaned.

The teacher cleared his throat. "Girls," he said, staring in their direction. "Is there something you'd like to tell the class?"

"No, sir," Halle and Izzy answered together, embarrassed to be caught talking.

"Well then, might I suggest you turn your attention back to revision and the importance of eliminating excessive adverbs?"

Izzy smiled respectfully at the teacher. "Yes, sir."

Halle flicked her finger down her nose. "Brownnoser," she whispered, teasing Izzy's eagerness.

Fifty-five minutes later, the class bell rang.

"Come on, let's go talk where we won't be interrupted," Halle said, linking her arm through Izzy's.

Izzy stopped, reaching down to pull the phone from her knee sock, which lit with an incoming text from Jacob.

"Just a sec," Izzy said, her face softening. "Sorry."

Halle rolled her head to the side, stretching the knotted muscles as Izzy typed her reply.

"Jacob wants my help before inter-house dodgeball. I guess the guys in Drake are painting their entire faces red and they need help. You want to come? Please? You'll have fun! I promise we can talk as soon as we're done."

Halle puffed out her cheeks, blowing the air through her lips. "No, that's okay. I'm not feeling super social."

Izzy looked disappointed. "No problem. I'll tell Jacob I'll see him at the game."

"No, Iz, go. You don't need me."

"Yeah, but I don't want to ditch you, either. You've kind of had the day from hell."

"I'm fine, really," Halle said, waving her away. "Go be with your boyfriend. I wouldn't mind being by myself for a bit anyway. I'll tell you everything when you get back. Don't worry."

"Are you sure?"

"Go!"

Izzy smiled. "Love you, roomie."

"Love you too."

After a brief hug, Izzy bounced away.

Wyatt waited for Halle, leaning against the wall in the hall before falling in stride with her as she left. They walked together in silence until they reached the outer doors of the English building.

"Hey," Wyatt said as they stepped outside.

"Hey."

"So, anything happen after lunch?"

"Well, your ex-girlfriend Missy accosted me again. Then I was pulled out of class, accused of having drugs on my person, and told to pee in a cup." Halle sucked in a breath. "I'd say my afternoon went according to plan."

"Shit, sorry. That sucks."

"What, Missy? Or the fact that the school thinks I'm high on crack?"

"Both, and it was cocaine. They're a little different."

"God, I've never even smoked pot! This is so messed up."

Wyatt nodded. "Yeah, I know how you feel, actually."

"How?" Halle said, briefly forgetting what Alex had told her.

"My mother just married this politician, and because I messed up once he thinks I'm going to do it again. Neither of them believes a word I say. All they care about these days is that I don't embarrass them. They make me do a drug test every week. So yeah, I think I know how you feel."

"God, I'm sorry, Wyatt." Halle felt like an ass.

"Alex is the only other person on campus who knows, besides Mr. Scott. I'd like to keep it that way."

"I promise I won't say a thing." Halle felt honored that Wyatt trusted her enough to share that about himself. She slowed her pace. "Wyatt, I still want to bring these guys down. What they did to me, what they did to Alex, it's not right."

"Yeah, I'm with you."

"Any word on when Jasper is making the buy?"

"Sometime tonight, that's all I know."

"Good."

CHAPTER 53

Screams echoed off the gymnasium walls, rattling Halle's thoughts. Her skin itched in anticipation of the next rubber ball. She caught it as it spun her way, then flung the ball back over the red centerline, smacking Sue, a grade 10 girl, right in the center of her back. Halle almost felt guilty. She shouldn't pick on girls who only came up to her shoulders, regardless of the competitive nature of the game. She tried to wave as Sue limped off but didn't think the girl saw her. Another ball whooshed by, barely missing Halle's leg. The timer buzzed. Halle, along with four others from her house, survived, and having the most players left on the court, Campbell House advanced to the next round. The girls from Windsor House were officially out of the tournament.

Halle slapped the hands of the remaining girls as their captain motioned for the team to gather round.

"Great job, guys. Be back in thirty minutes. We play the winners of the next game for first place."

Halle tugged her sweatshirt over her head.

"Hey," Wyatt said, weaving through the crowd. His tight black jeans cuffed above light suede loafers seemed grossly out of place in the sweat-filled gym.

"Hi, Wyatt," Halle said, laughing. "Where did you come from?"

"I was in the stands. Good game."

"Showing a little school spirit?" Halle teased, placing her hand against her chest. "What's gotten into you? You're not feeling sick or anything?"

"Shut up," Wyatt said, but Halle could tell he was laughing. "Actually, for your information, I'm keeping an eye out for Jasper."

"Really?" Halle asked, turning serious. "Where is he?"

"Over there." Wyatt pointed to the bleachers.

Halle wiped her sweaty face with a sports towel left by the school trainer.

"What are you doing now that your game is over?" Wyatt asked.

"First, I'm finding my sweatpants. Then, I guess I'm watching the next game. What about you?"

Before Wyatt could answer, Izzy came over, dragging Jacob behind her. "Hi, guys."

"Hey, Izzy," Wyatt said, nodding at the pair. "Jacob."

Izzy smiled. "You guys want to go grab a soda or something before the next round of games?"

"Sure," said Wyatt, surprising Halle.

"Cool."

"Will someone help me find my pants," Halle said, combing the bleachers for her sweats.

"These them?" Izzy held up a pair of familiar deep purple school sweats.

"Thanks!"

The alarm on Wyatt's phone sounded, stopping Halle in her tracks.

"Come on," Izzy said and headed through the main doors of the gym.

Wyatt looked down at his screen, then jerked his head toward the bleachers. "Jasper's leaving."

Halle winced. "We'll see you in a second, Iz. Something just came up."

CHAPTER 54

Wyatt fired up the tracking app before letting Jasper leave his line of sight. "Got him."

Halle looked down at Wyatt's phone. "Sweet."

"You sure you're ready for this? I could just meet up with you later. Tell you how things went down. That way Alex won't kill me when he finds out what we're up to," Wyatt said, hoping Halle would agree.

"No way you're gonna leave without me."

Jasper entered the woods on the other side of the rugby pitch opposite the gymnasium, the thick evergreen forest swallowing him immediately.

Halle flipped Wyatt's hand over, checking to make sure the tracker still pinged his location. "Let's go."

The ground, damp underfoot, soaked through her canvas court shoes instantly. Halle grimaced as her toes swam, sticking together in her wet socks. "Remind me to wear boots next time," she whispered.

"Next time?" Wyatt scoffed, not turning.

Fallen twigs crunched beneath their feet while low-lying branches caught on their clothes and snapped as they pushed through them. An owl hooted, making Halle shudder just as Wyatt slipped on a moss-covered rock, barely catching his balance.

"Maybe you should consider wearing boots too."

"Whatever," he growled.

The glowing red dot representing Jasper turned left for a few hundred meters and then right for the next half a kilometer.

"Any idea where we're going?" Halle asked. It was spooky and difficult trying to keep up with Jasper in the dark woods.

The trail turned steep, climbing the hill behind campus. "My money's on the housing development up on the crest. There's a bit of an old deer trail over here. Follow me."

"I think this is where Leigh used to run," Halle whispered as the trail evened out.

"Who's Leigh?"

"A good friend. She graduated my grade eight year. She's—"

Wyatt extended his arm, stopping Halle from going farther. In the distance, Halle could see an opening in the woods where the trail stopped.

"We're here," Wyatt whispered.

CHAPTER 55

At the end of the rough path they'd been following stood a tall standard aluminum street lamp illuminating a quiet cul-de-sac. Three of the five houses surrounding the empty street showed signs of life: interior lights, crossing shadows, movement behind curtains.

"It looks like he went into the house over there," Wyatt said, peering down at the tracker and then pointing to a medium-size one-level tract home backed up to the forestlands, with a barren yard and peeling yellow paint. The white retracting garage door was open, and a covered car sat nestled between standing toolboxes, unpacked moving boxes, and a long wooden shop table.

Halle nodded in agreement, following as he made his way to the closest exterior wall of the garage. As they passed the open door, Halle stared at a glimpse of chrome and black exposed by the corner of the brown canvas cover snagged on the car's taillight. Something about the car seemed familiar, but then again, after spending so much time around Alex, most cars did. This one made Halle think the car was vintage, 1960s maybe. Alex would know if he were here. A corner of the license plate read *Sunshine* in bright green.

Voices inside the house escalated. "Over there," Wyatt said, pulling Halle along. At the back of the house, just past the side of the garage, was a dark alcove beneath a lit window. From where they crouched, Halle could see the street, but she doubted anyone could see them.

"How much do you need?" a man yelled through the house.

Wyatt heard Jasper's voice coming from the room above their heads. "I have a buyer who wants an ounce of BC Gold, plus the usual."

The man snorted. "You kids getting picky about your bud now?" Jasper didn't answer, but they could hear someone shuffling about the room. "You got the cash?"

A couple more minutes passed before the door from the house to the garage opened. Jasper walked out past the car and left. Wyatt nodded to Halle, motioning for her to follow him just as a second person entered the room above them.

They heard a woman's voice say, "I don't like you selling to the students, Ramon."

Halle yanked Wyatt back under the window.

"You worry too much, Lola. The kid needs us more than we need him. No one else in the valley will sell to him. I've made sure of it. We're all the greedy little bastard has."

Halle gave Wyatt a knowing look.

"We got other problems, too," Lola said. "That girl Halle never got the boot today. I stuck the coke in her pack at lunch. Talked real loud to one of ladies in the teacher's lounge when I went to clean up. Even double-checked to see if anything was happening in the office after classes when I brought a tray of cookies up there. They found nothing, but they liked the baked goods."

"Shh—" Wyatt covered her mouth with his hand before Halle could do more than gasp.

Halle's heart stopped, then started slamming against her rib cage.

Lola continued, "I think she's on to us. We're going to have to try something else in a couple of days or we need to hightail it out of here."

Ramon cursed. "I'm not running till I finish this sale, Lola. Finding a buyer for all the coke took me two years. We're not going anywhere till this deal goes down. Eight days, Lola, that's all I need. Just give me a week."

"I don't know. I got a bad feeling about this. Let's just take the rest of the school's food money and get out of here. With what we've pulled from the accounts already we could go down to Mexico, find someone else to buy."

The sound of a fist slamming against the counter vibrated through the air.

"No! We got a good thing here, woman! I'm not letting some snot-nosed kid get in the middle of it. How do I even know you got the coke in the right backpack? Them things all look the same. Could be some kid walking around right now with a bag of my shit having the time of his life. The way I see it, you and your damn paranoia just cost me a lot of money. We're hanging tight. End of discussion."

"You're a goddamn idiot, Ramon. I hope you end up in jail."

"If you keep this up, you're the next one going for a swim off a ferry."

Told you, Halle mouthed.

Wyatt vowed never to doubt Halle again.

The voices petered out, and soon the light in the window was switched off.

Wyatt eased away from their hiding spot.

Halle didn't move.

Wyatt's brow furrowed.

"What license plate has *Sunshine* on it?" Halle whispered.

"What? I don't know!" Wyatt reached for Halle's arm. Roughly pulling her behind him, they headed back toward the woods.

The door between the house and the garage opened, and the florescent work lights above the car blazed.

Halle tugged her arm free. "When I was little we used to play this game with my family whenever we went on a road trip. The person who spotted the most state plates won an ice cream bar."

"So?"

"So, the car in the garage had a license that had *Sunshine* printed on it. If the plate is from Florida, like I'm guessing, my uncle can trace the numbers, make the connection, and finally have to listen to me."

"We are not going back there, Halle. Not tonight, not ever."

"What the hell do you mean? We can solve this! We can bust a murderer. We can clear Alex's name."

"Call your uncle!"

"He won't listen!"

Wyatt peered back through the trees at the Riveros' garage. Ramon lifted the car cover, opened the hood, and bent over the engine box.

"No," Wyatt said. "Not when they're here. It's too dangerous. We don't even know if the plates are from Florida yet. Until we figure this out, you have to lay low. Like really low, Halle. You heard Lola. They're on to you. Throw out your pack. From now on you're carrying your books."

CHAPTER 56

"Where the hell have you been?" Izzy yelled as Halle opened the door to their room.

"You wouldn't believe me if I told you."

"Try me!"

Mud stains covered Halle's legs while an angry red scratch crossed her cheek.

"And while you're explaining things, you might want add where the hell that scratch came from. You look like you lost a fight."

"Thanks."

"Seriously, Hal, what the hell is going on? I came back here to talk to you after the last game, which by the way we lost because you failed to show up."

Halle closed her eyes, hating the fact that she let her team down. "Listen, Iz, I'm sorry. I want to tell you everything and I will, but I have to take a shower and eat something before my blood sugar bottoms out. I don't want to go all postal on your ass."

Izzy dug through her food drawer, throwing a cookie-dough-flavored protein bar at her roommate.

Halle's hand shot out and caught it. "Thanks."

Fifteen minutes later, Halle walked out of the bathroom sporting clean puppy-print pajamas.

"I'm waiting," Izzy said, sitting cross-legged on her bed.

"If I'm going to get into this, I'm only explaining things once." Halle opened her computer and dialed Alex's number on iChat.

"Hey," Alex said, his eyes half closed. "Iz, is that you, too? You better not be calling after some kind of party. I swear, if you are I'm hanging up." Alex pressed his hand to his mouth, stifling a yawn. "Hal, what's up with your face?"

Halle pressed her palm to her forehead. "I scraped my cheek running into a tree. But more importantly, I know who planted the drugs in your pack."

Alex clicked on his bedside lamp. Izzy eye's bulged.

"Wyatt and I followed Jasper when he went to go buy pot tonight."

Izzy coughed, choking as she tried to swallow. "Excuse me?"

"What the hell, Halle!" Alex yelled, his face turning red.

"Alex, I found cocaine in my backpack after lunch today."

The twins' jaws dropped.

"It was in my pencil bag. Wyatt was there and helped me get rid of it. By the time I was called into Mr. Davies's office everything was gone, but I had to take a test and they searched our room."

"Why didn't you say anything?" Izzy yelled. "This is my room too!"

"I tried, remember? You blew me off for Jacob. Then, I didn't say anything at the dodgeball game because I didn't think the timing was right. You would've freaked out in the gym, so don't even go there."

Alex cleared his throat, interrupting Halle and his sister. "Why did you follow Jasper?"

Halle took several deep breaths, cracking each knuckle in her right hand before continuing. "I went to help Mrs. Middleton in the library last week. She wanted me to organize her desk, so she sent me down to the kitchen to grab zip bags to organize the stuff in her desk with. When I finally found where the bags were kept I found this." Halle reached into the shallow bottom drawer of her desk and pulled out a crinkled wax paper sandwich bag.

Alex covered his mouth with his hand, rubbing the stubble on his chin with his fingers. "No way," he said through his fingers.

"I don't get it," Izzy said.

"It's the same type the pot was in that was planted in my bag."

"So I did the only thing I could think of. I ran to Wyatt."

Alex frowned.

"Don't give me that look," Halle warned.

"Why the hell would you run to Wyatt?"

"Because I assumed they were his drugs in the first place. I don't know, somehow going to him made sense to me at the time. I'm glad I did, though. He wants you back on campus almost as much as I do."

Alex shook his head, hardly believing what he was hearing. "Continue."

"I told him everything. How you saw the guy get killed on the ferry. What I found on the Internet. He listened and he agreed with me. Something you haven't really been willing to do."

"I'm going to kill him."

"No, you're not."

"Jesus, Hal," Alex barked.

"Anyway, Wyatt thought if we could figure out where the pot came from, it might lead us to who planted it on you in the first place, even though I was already pretty sure the Riveros were responsible."

"So what did you do?" Izzy asked.

"We followed him through the woods behind the rugby fields into a housing development on top of the hill. To the Riveros' house. After Jasper left and we were starting to leave, Lola came into the room. She and Ramon started arguing, and we heard it all. The murder, the drug deal in Florida, everything. They're selling the cocaine sometime soon, then they're blowing out of town."

"Halle—" Alex began.

"Oh yeah, and there's a reason the food sucks. They've been stealing cash from the food budget until they can sell the coke. That's why they're freaking out so much and why the food here stinks. I'll bet the garbage they're serving us isn't even prison grade."

"This is so not happening!" Alex yelled.

"I'm sorry, Hal, Alex is right. This is crazy." Izzy popped to her feet and paced behind Halle's chair.

"No, you guys don't understand," Halle insisted, tears rapidly gathering in the corners of her eyes. "The police aren't listening to me. You guys have to."

"No!" Alex roared. "You need to let this go, Halle. These guys are murderers! Your life is in danger! I don't give a crap about coming back to campus if it means you're involved in something like this."

CHAPTER 57

Alex punched his pillow for the umpteenth time, trying to get comfortable. His mind raced along with his pulse. How could he have let things with Halle get this out of control? This was his mess, his problem. Halle trying to fix it didn't surprise him, but the lengths she was willing to go unsettled him to no end.

He picked up his phone and texted his sister.

•

April 17, 2015 11:57 PM

Alex: Iz you up?

    Izzy: Yeah, little hard to sleep.

Alex: No kidding.

    Izzy: What's up?

Alex: I'm freaking out.

    Izzy: Yeah, me too. This whole thing is crazy.

Alex: You're telling me.

    Izzy: I'm kind of scared Alex. If the Riveros suspect Halle's on to them, they might think I am too. Are they going to come after me?

Alex: I don't know. I'm sorry Iz! I never meant for this to happen.

    Izzy: I know. We'll figure this out. I know we will. I just keep thinking about tomorrow. I'm afraid to go to breakfast. I just want to come home.

Alex: Is there anyone at school we can talk to?

    Izzy: I don't think anyone will believe us. Halle's tried to talk to her uncle but he says there's not enough evidence for him to do anything. Without

Nico's body, nothing links the murder you saw with the Riveros being drug dealers.

Alex: Can we call Blakely?

Izzy: No way. Halle'd kill us. We can't call Max either or her parents. She made me promise not to get them involved.

Alex: We can't do nothing!

Izzy: There is one person she didn't mention, but I don't know.

Alex: Who???? Iz, this is serious. You have to tell me.

Izzy: She didn't say anything about North.

Alex: North?

Izzy: Yeah. He lives with Max and Blakely. He might know what to do. At the very least, he could talk to Blakely for us.

CHAPTER 58

After texting Izzy, Alex jumped out of bed. His hair stuck out in a hundred different directions. He looked crazy and felt crazed. He started pacing the length of his room. The frustration, anger, and overwhelming sense of helplessness ricocheting around his head made him dizzy.

From his Facebook page, Alex found the number to the one person Halle hadn't made them promise not to contact. He picked up his phone. Oblivious to the time, Alex punched the numbers in and waited for the call to connect.

"Hello?"

The deep, sleepy voice answering the phone hit Alex in the gut. Halle admitted to crushing on the guy for years. The thought of her interested in someone besides him made Alex's blood boil. He had never met North, just knew of him through stories told by Halle and her sister. Some kind of rugby star and her big sister's best friend, who practically lived with them when he attended Lakeview with Blakely.

"Hi, um, my name is Alex Dumas. I'm a friend of Halle Henry."

"Morning, Alex. I know who you are. What can I do for you?"

Alex took a deep breath, dragging the hand not clutching the phone through his hair. He didn't know where to start.

"I think Halle's in trouble."

North's end of the line went silent. "Hold on a second." In the background, Alex could hear sheets rustling and realized it was just after eight o'clock in the morning where North lived. "Okay, now what the hell are you talking about?"

Alex started at the beginning, telling North everything that had happened.

"Hold on there, mate. You're telling me Halle's gotten wrapped up with a pair of drug dealers from Florida who've committed a murder? Bloody hell."

"She tried to go to her uncle, but he can't do anything without more proof. She doesn't think he'll even listen to her, plus she knows the school won't do a thing because the people involved in this are staff members."

"Why hasn't she called her sister?"

"She says she doesn't want to be a buzz kill, whatever that means."

North thought of Blakely and Max announcing their engagement and didn't blame Halle for not wanting to interrupt their happily-ever-after, but Jesus Christ. This was a mess. Halle should have called him with this before this kid did. Now he would have to tell Blakely, because Halle needed her help, whether she wanted assistance or not. There were certain perks to being the figurehead of a small country; having your own secret service was one of them.

"I didn't know what else to do. Can you help me help her?"

"Yeah," North answered. "But when I'm done I'm going to kill your girlfriend."

"Get in line."

CHAPTER 59

Halle's sheets tangled around her legs, trapping her. She felt like she was falling, her breath coming in quick gulps. Beads of sweat covered her brow. It's just a dream, she told herself, forcing her eyes open. Izzy's soft breathing brought Halle back to reality. Her body ached from the night before. She'd physically shut down when Alex started yelling at her. As soon as the video call ended, she had crawled beneath her comforter, falling to sleep within minutes.

Sitting up now, she looked into the darkness. She hated having the blinds drawn at night, claiming the natural light made it easier to wake in the mornings, but in truth, since grade 8, she'd been afraid of the dark. Somehow, the bits of light that drifted through their window from the main campus made it easier for her to sleep.

Halle brought the back of her hand up against her forehead. Her skin felt clammy, not hot. She didn't feel like she had a fever but she was shaking.

The car. How could she have forgotten to look up the license plate? *Sunshine . . .*

Alex's warning echoed in her ears, but she ignored it. No one would believe her if she didn't have proof that the Riveros were in fact the Perezes, and if Lola and Ramon skipped town before the police pieced things together she knew they'd never find them again. Halle pulled her computer to her lap, resting it against her legs. The time in the top corner of the information bar read 2:54 a.m. She typed "State license plate logos" into the Google search bar. Pressing on the Images tag, she scrolled down the page. Dozens of pictures danced across the screen. Several rows down, Halle's hand stilled as she found what she'd been looking for: a plate with an orange branch perched in the center. Halle read the bold green writing: Sunshine State, Florida.

CHAPTER 60

St. Andrews, Scotland

When North first heard the kid's voice, he'd been annoyed, but when Halle's boyfriend said she was in trouble, his gut twisted and he jumped out of bed. He wished Halle had called him. He thought of her as a sister. Sure, in the last couple years they'd drifted apart a bit. With his sport commitments he rarely saw her. Had it been two years? He couldn't remember. When she started dating this Alex guy the calls stopped coming on a regular basis. The thought stung. They were still Facebook friends, though, but man.

North stroked the stubble on his chin. How did Halle always end up over her head in things she shouldn't be involved with in the first place? He knew as soon as she started dating this guy that Alex would never be man enough to protect her. North grabbed his watch from the bedside table, groaning at the early hour. "Bloody hell!" He reached for his sweats.

North lived in the basement suite of his best friend's fiancé's house.

Fiancé. The word felt strange to him. But Blakely and Max had the real thing. He was happy for them. North doubted he'd ever be that lucky. The string of women he hung out with never seemed to fit what he thought was marriage material. After a few dates they all seemed to bore him. What was the point of being bored at twenty-two?

"Dude, you up?" he yelled, banging on the door to the apartment above his. The security guard waved to North from his post at the gate. Since Queen Blakely spent most of her time at Max's house, certain security measures had been put in place. North waved back to the guard, jealous of the steaming mug of coffee he held in his hands.

"Max!" North shouted, growing impatient. "Wake the hell up and answer the goddamn door!"

"Piss off," Max said, cracking the door just enough to see out. He snarled at North. "Do you know what time it is?"

"Yes! Now open up."

Max rubbed the sleep from his eyes. "You better have a good reason for waking me up."

"Let me in or I'll beat the crap out of you. It's freezing out here. How's that for a reason?"

Max laughed, allowing North entry. "Now, what is going on?"

"Where's Blake?"

"Upstairs asleep."

"You better wake her."

Blakely padded down the stairs in a pair of pink pajama bottoms with a well-worn University of Washington sweatshirt she'd owned since living in Washington State draped over her loose tank top, her hair up in a tangled bun. She gave an appreciative smile to the two shirtless men in her kitchen. North leaned against the counter. He was a couple inches taller than Max, with a thicker chest and broader shoulders, but both of them could stop traffic.

"Morning," she said, her voice still thick with sleep. "What's going on?"

Max smiled as Blakely walked into his welcoming arms, nestling herself into his warm embrace.

North took a deep breath. "Your sister's in trouble."

CHAPTER 61

Lakeview Academy

Vancouver Island, British Columbia

Halle touched the scratch on her cheek. The swollen red gash stood out against her pale skin. She looked over at Izzy, still sleeping soundly, feeling a twang of jealousy. Covering her face with her pillow, she willed herself to go back to sleep. What good were Saturdays if not to sleep in longer than usual? Within minutes, though, she threw her pillow from her bed, giving up.

She knew what she needed to do after finding the Florida license plate last night, yet before ending the iChat with Alex, she made a promise to both him and Izzy that she would leave things alone. Alex even threatened to break up with her if she didn't listen, claiming he couldn't date someone who would put themselves in dangerous situations like this. Halle took a deep breath, exhaling loudly. Sometimes Alex could be so dramatic. He actually warned her, "Don't make me not trust you, Halle."

"Screw that," Halle cursed, sliding from the warm fold of her blankets. He would forgive her when he was back on campus with her, where he belonged. Even be grateful.

"Where are you going?" Izzy asked groggily as Halle grabbed a pair of old yoga pants from the floor of her closet.

"The bathroom." Halle pulled on her heaviest wool socks, sighing as they heated her toes back up to normal body temperature. Was the window open, she wondered, wrapping her arms around her chest. "Damn, it's cold in here."

Izzy opened one eye, peering from the cocoon of her aqua-blue tie-dyed sheets. "No, you're not. You're headed out."

"Yeah, but I have to brush my teeth first."

"Okay, after you brush your teeth where are you going?"

"I thought I'd go find Wyatt."

Izzy swore under her breath. "Why?"

"I saw something last night. I want to talk to him about it."

Izzy slipped from her bed.

"What are you doing?" Halle asked.

"Coming with you."

Halle scrunched her face up. "Why the hell do you want to do that?"

"I don't, but you promised me you'd stop looking into the Riveros. Finding Wyatt doesn't sound like you're leaving things alone, so I'm going with you."

"Like hell you are."

"You wanna bet?"

"So, what, you're like my babysitter now?"

"If that's what it takes."

Defeated, Halle fell back onto her bed. "I can't believe you."

"Look who's talking."

CHAPTER 62

April 18, 2015 9:32 AM

Halle: We need to talk.

    Wyatt: Hello to you too.

Halle: Wyatt, be serious.

    Wyatt: I am.

Halle: I told Izzy & Alex about what we did last night.

    Wyatt: I know. I got a rather pissy call from your boyfriend. He's seriously upset with me. Says this is all my fault.

Halle: Well he's pissed at me too if that helps. He really told you this was your fault?

    Wyatt: Yup.

Halle: Screw that. Does he not remember that he was the idiot who witnessed a murder?

    Wyatt: You took the words right out of my mouth.

Halle: Well if it makes you feel any better he & Izzy have put me under house arrest.

    Wyatt: ???

Halle: I tried to go over to see you this morning & Izzy wouldn't let me leave. I'm actually typing from the bathroom right now so she won't catch me texting you.

    Wyatt: Hahaha

Halle: Not funny.

    Wyatt: She got you chained up or anything?

Halle: No

    Wyatt: Then ditch her.

Halle: Not really an easy thing to do right now.

Wyatt: Why did you need to see me?

Halle: The plate I saw last night is from Florida. I'm sure of it. They're the only plate with the word sunshine. We have to go back.

Wyatt: Seriously? Do you have a death wish?

Halle: It's just a picture. I'll do it with or without your help. Your choice.

CHAPTER 63

Wyatt caught up to Halle on the quad, her roommate by her side. "So what's the plan?"

"Nothing's the plan," Izzy said, glaring.

"Jesus, Izzy, don't get your panties in a bunch," said Wyatt. "I didn't start this. Did she tell you what she wants to do now?"

"No," Izzy snarled, crossing her arms over her chest.

Halle looked to the sky and took several deep breaths.

"I thought you were done keeping secrets," Izzy said.

"I am."

"It's actually not that bad of an idea," said Wyatt.

Izzy turned to him, her expression hardened with anger. "Whatever it is, she's not doing it."

Halle's patience with her roommate's overprotective behavior evaporated. "Iz, you can't really expect me to do nothing. Your brother's future is at stake, there's over a million dollars worth of cocaine that might hit the streets, there's an unsolved murder, plus, on top of it all, a bunch of school money has been stolen. And you seriously just want to let that ride and take a chance that someone else is going to catch these guys before it's too late?"

Izzy shifted her weight from one foot to the other, uncrossed her arms, and planted her left hand on her hip.

"We just need a photograph."

Izzy's face softened slightly. "Explain."

Halle told her how she looked up the plates and how having a picture would give her uncle what he needed to look into things a bit more seriously.

"How the hell do you sleep through this crap?" Wyatt asked.

Izzy shrugged. "Lucky, I guess?"

"And I thought I had the bad end of the deal rooming with Alex."

Halle whacked Wyatt's shoulder with the back of her hand. "Come on, Iz. You want to help or are we doing this without you?"

Izzy loved her brother but everything Halle just told her made sense. If Alex were here he would see that. She knew it. Izzy took a slow deep breath. The pros of doing something now clearly outnumbered the cons. "I'll only help if you do this when we know the Riveros are on campus, not at home. I don't want to take any more chances."

"Agreed," Wyatt said.

Halle nodded. "So when do we do it?"

All three stood there, deep in thought. The wind picked up, swirling cherry blossoms into the air around them.

"Tomorrow, before dinner," Izzy said, picking at a petal that landed on her sweater.

"She's right. Meals are optional on Saturday night because the Riveros have the day off."

"How do you know that?" Halle asked.

"Food's always better when they aren't here," Wyatt said, shrugging.

"You *cannot* tell Alex about this," Halle said, pointing at Izzy.

"Hal's right. If you tell him, he's liable to go off, making things worse for everyone. We don't want these assholes to get away with what they've done."

"Don't even tell Jacob," Halle said, wagging her finger in the air. "We've got to keep this to just the three of us."

Izzy nodded. "I can't believe you talked me into this."

CHAPTER 64

Edinburgh, Scotland

North mounted the stairs to the private jet, fueled up and ready to leave, on the tarmac at the Edinburgh Airport. He, Blakely, and Max were meeting Blakely's parents at Paris's de Gaulle airport in less than three hours. From there they would continue straight to Victoria. They should be at Lakeview by tomorrow afternoon at the latest.

He ran his calloused hands down his jaw. He needed a beer, maybe two. He already knew he wouldn't be able to sleep. He rarely slept on planes, figuring they would never crash as long as he kept his eyes open. Sometimes he laughed at his own stupid superstitions, but hey, if it worked it worked. Why mess with it. He'd never been in a plane wreck yet.

Blakely took her seat opposite Max and across the aisle from North on the Gulfstream G5, the deep leather seats welcoming her tense body.

"It'll be okay," Max assured her.

North was skeptical. He, like Blakely, knew Halle a little better than Max did. He tried to remember the first time he met her. Four years and five grades separated them. North had always been the youngest in his grade, after skipping grade 7. No one ever guessed, however, because of his size. He stopped growing in grade 8, hitting six foot two. In grade 10, he weighed 210 pounds, thanks to his rugby coach's weight-lifting program. He would have been thirteen years old, he concluded. Halle had been the skinniest little kid back then, driving Mrs. Henry—Lili, as she made him call her—crazy with her bad eating habits. If he remembered right, she only ate yellow things that year: mac and cheese, quesadillas, pasta, and butter. The thought made him smile.

Halle always took unchecked risks. He remembered one weekend helping her father retrieve her from the side of the house where she had managed to free climb up the outside of the stone chimney, reaching the second floor before getting stuck.

"Did you get ahold of your uncle?" Max asked.

"No, but Mom did. I've never heard her so mad. I kind of feel sorry for him."

The flight attendant opened a bottle of beer, poured it into a frosted glass, and passed it to North. Minutes later, he looked out the window as the ground below them disappeared. A deep groan came from the back of North's throat. "Is he going to meet us on campus?"

"Yes, Dad had Duncan call in an international favor. The RCMP's Drug Enforcement Branch is involved, as well as the local police, and Uncle Mike is going to be leading a second team of officers from West Vancouver. The last thing I heard before I boarded the plane was that the RCMP confirmed Halle's suspicions regarding the Riveros after doing a background search of their own. They're going to set up surveillance units outside their house until they can determine when the deal is going to go down so that they can bust the buyer at the same time.

"No one's telling Halle about this until we get there, right? Just in case. To keep her safe."

"Right, or the school. They want everything as normal as possible. The last thing we want is for the Riveros to get wind of what's going on and do something stupid."

North took a sip of his beer. The cold bubbles exploded in his mouth. "Good."

CHAPTER 65

The trail behind campus leading to the Riveros' looked completely different in the dimming light of dusk. Behind them, Mr. Scott blew his whistle, calling for an end to the rugby practices taking place on the fields below.

"I can't believe you did this in the dark," Izzy hissed, pulling a thorny vine from her sleeve, the back of her hands already marked with several long pink lines that would surely be infected by morning.

The gray evening, common in the spring on Vancouver Island, wrapped around them, thick with the coming rain Halle knew would start at any minute. In another month the blue skies would show themselves on a daily basis; not now, though. April showers bring May flowers, wasn't that the old expression? Halle bit back a laugh thinking that. April showers brought moss but that was about it. The cul-de-sac appeared through the trees, all five houses looking ghostlike in the gloomy evening light.

"Is that it?" Izzy asked, pointing to the fading yellow house that had seen better days.

Halle nodded. The night before, Wyatt and Halle described the area in detail, so Izzy knew what she was heading into.

Wyatt pressed his finger to his lips and waved his hand, indicating that the girls should follow him as he took the lead. Instead of walking along the street, as they had done the first night, Wyatt wove through the tree line. They didn't wear camouflage, none of them owned any, but they did do their best to blend in. "No bright colors or identifying school logos," Wyatt warned them the night before, so the girls chose black leggings, navy-blue hoodies and sneakers, in case they needed to run. Even Wyatt went without the flashy clothes he loved, choosing a black tracksuit that made Halle giggle when she saw him. She teased him mercilessly until they reached the school side of the trail and started into the woods.

A plumbing van with "Mel's Pump & Dump" painted on the side sat quietly on the street across from the Riveros' garage. A new white pickup that Halle didn't see the night before was parked in the driveway of the gray house two doors to the right.

"Don't get seen by the neighbors," Wyatt whispered, assessing the street scene. It was busier looking than he'd anticipated.

"Is that the car?" Izzy whispered, pointing to the flat-black Dodge Charger parked in the driveway.

"No," said Halle. She pointed to the white garage door. "The car we want's in there."

"Inside the garage?"

Halle nodded.

"But the door's closed," Izzy said.

"Yup, looks that way."

Izzy's nose scrunched. "Then whose car is that?"

Halle shrugged. "Are we sure the Riveros aren't home?"

"Yes," Wyatt said. "I checked Mason Hall right before we left. They were both there."

Halle took a deep breath. "How do we get in?"

"There," Wyatt said, pointing.

Halle followed his raised index finger to the garage's side door, not too far from where they crouched hidden in the shadows two nights before.

Halle nodded. "Do you think it's unlocked?"

"Doesn't matter." Wyatt held out a credit card. "I can get us in."

Halle gaped in surprise. "You can pick locks?"

"I wasn't exactly the best kid at my old school. I guess I've given my mum a thing or two to worry about over the years after all. As long as there isn't a secondary bolt, I can jimmy the thing."

"Okay, I take back every mean thing I ever said about you. You're awesome!"

"Are you guys smoking something I'm not aware of?" Izzy spat. "This is crazy."

"We can be in and out in less than a minute," Halle said. "No big deal."

"We can't break into the Riveros' house."

"We're not breaking into their house," Wyatt said. "Just the garage."

Izzy shook her head. "No way!"

Halle and Wyatt looked at the door, then back to the other with a shrug.

"You should stay here, Izzy," Wyatt said. "Someone needs to watch the house and warn us if anyone approaches."

Izzy swallowed loudly. "I can't believe we're doing this."

"It's not like we have much of a choice," said Halle. "I'll grab the picture, then this whole thing is over. We can go back to normal. Alex too."

Izzy placed her hand on her roommate's arm. "Be careful."

Halle nodded.

Wyatt looked at Izzy. "Do you know how to whistle?"

"You did not just ask her that," Halle moaned. "Seriously, Wyatt, how many old movies do you watch? Whistling is beyond cliché. Plus it's stupid." Halle reached down and grabbed a jagged rock around the size of a hockey puck. "Take this.

"Remember playing softball with us last summer?" Halle said, passing the stone to Izzy. "Your aim is unreal. Go hide over there, close to that tree. Throw this at us if you see anyone approaching the house."

Izzy nodded.

"Ready?" Halle said, glancing back over at Wyatt.

"Let's do this."

CHAPTER 66

Halle checked for Izzy. Izzy waved once in position, crouching behind a large maple tree. The first sprinkling of rain started falling.

"Over here," Wyatt said, finding the best route to the garage's side door through the trees at the back of the Riveros' uncut yard. "You first."

Halle's foot sank into a puddle of mud. "Ew. Tell me they don't have a dog, because I swear that wasn't dirt I just stepped in, plus a pit bull would really mess with this plan."

Wyatt's wide mouth sported a lopsided grin. "I don't hear barking, and I didn't see anything the other night. I think we're good."

Halle wasn't entirely convinced.

Bending low at the waist, they sprinted across the small patchy lawn. With a nod, Wyatt tested the knob on the white door at the side of the garage. It turned easily in his hand. His brows rose.

"Lucky."

"Get your camera ready," Wyatt said.

Halle grabbed the hard plastic sides of her iPhone case in the kangaroo pocket of her dark blue sweatshirt. She slid her finger across the home screen and pressed the camera icon, checking the image orientation. "Okay."

Wyatt eased the door open. The dirt-streaked glass of the side door's small window allowed them to see only shadows.

"Did you bring a flashlight?" Halle whispered.

"Shit," Wyatt swore. The paint can he just ran into rattled on its edge, threatening to tip over before sitting still and quiet again.

A glow flooded through the gap at the base of the door into the house. Someone had just switched on the light.

"Get behind the car," Wyatt hissed, pushing Halle forward before ducking behind the refrigerator in the corner.

The door between the house and the garage opened. "You hear something out here?"

Holding her breath, Halle pressed herself against the car, sliding her body around to the back end.

The aluminum panels of the garage door started rolling up. The man standing in the doorway to the house cursed. "Goddamnit! I think this cheap-ass opener just shocked me. Where's the damn light?"

Peering around the corner of the car, Halle noticed a long, thick scar spanning the side of the man's shiny bald head, just above his left ear. A thin mustache curled up then trailed down the corners of his mouth, meeting with a neatly trimmed beard the color of soot.

"How much longer till Ramon gets back?" the bald man called back into the house. "This neighborhood gives me the creeps. It's too quiet."

"He said he'd be back around eight," a deeper voice answered from inside. "So we make the deal, then we get out of here. Grab me a cold one. Ramon said the beer's in the refrigerator out there."

Halle looked over her shoulder to Wyatt. If the man got any closer he would see him. She raised three fingers so Wyatt could see them counting down from three, then lifted the canvas cover near the trunk of the car. The faint sound of canvas brushing against metal filled the room. Halle snapped a picture of the license plate.

The man walking toward the refrigerator stopped.

Halle held her breath, clutching her phone to her chest.

"Hey, Dwayne!" the man in the garage yelled. "Come here!"

Wyatt reached for the paint container he'd just stumbled over and hurtled it at the man's head, hitting him square in the face. The man took a step back and fell to the floor.

"Run!" Wyatt yelled.

CHAPTER 67

Halle bolted out of the garage. Rain pounded on the ground around her.

Dwayne lunged through the kitchen door and almost tripped over his friend lying on the floor. "What the hell!" He spotted Halle running through the cul-de-sac and took off, his heavy footsteps thudding after her.

Across the street, the side door of the plumbing van opened. Several people spilled out, some running toward the yellow house, others toward the woods.

Halle's heart beat wildly, drowning out everything but the sound of her own feet hitting the ground. Reaching the tree line, she sprinted into the woods, praying that Dwayne was following her so that Wyatt and Izzy could get away and that Wyatt's actions had stalled Scarhead's ability to pursue either of them for at least the next few minutes. A branch behind her snapped loudly, urging her farther into the dense foliage. She pumped her arms and leaped over several moss-covered rocks. Twigs crunched underfoot as someone approached from her right. Halle felt disorientated, almost dizzy. Sweat and rain trickled down her cheeks. She ducked behind an old-growth cedar to hide, sinking to the base of the tree, trying to catch her breath.

Halle shoved the cell phone, still clutched in her hand, back into her bra. She couldn't lose the evidence now, not after everything her friends just did for her. She had to get the image of the license plate to her uncle. For the first time, Halle wished that she'd listened to him, but no, the thought of letting people like the Riveros go free made her gut clench.

More branches snapped from the opposite direction, this time closer to where she crouched. The sound of heavy breathing filled the air. Scrambling to her feet she started running again. Large hands, like steel vises, clamped down on her arms from behind.

Halle screamed, piercing the silence of the forest with her fear.

"I've got you! It's okay!"

Halle kept screaming, louder, her throat tightening, burning.

"Halle! Do you hear me?" The hands were shaking her now. "Halle! Look at me!" Her captor turned her, forcing her to face him.

Shocked, Halle gasped, gulping for air. "North?"

North pulled her against his chest. "I've got her! She's okay!" he yelled in the direction from which he came.

"North? But . . . how?" Halle couldn't believe her eyes. She buried her face into his neck, inhaling deeply. It was him, North. Halle knew his scent anywhere, pine and musk along with something else, so familiar that her knees wobbled.

"Hey," he cooed, kissing the top of her head.

"Wyatt, Izzy . . . ," Halle rasped.

North smiled, straight white teeth beneath full red lips. "We have them, too."

He stroked her hair, making Halle shiver as she let go of the adrenaline racing through her veins. He was so big, so warm. Halle never wanted to leave his embrace. "We? What 'we'? What . . . what are you doing here?"

North put his hands on either side of her face, curling his fingers through her loose hair, his thumbs caressing her cheeks.

"Alex called me."

"Alex?" Color flooded Halle's cheeks.

"He told me what was going on. You should have called me, Hal. I would have been here for you. I'll always be here for you."

Halle licked her lips, sucking the lower one between her teeth, making North groan and pull her back into his chest.

"You should have at least called your sister. She's been worried sick about you."

"I know." Halle sighed.

"Blake called your uncle. The police have been here since yesterday, watching the Riveros' house. The RCMP joined them this morning after getting the paperwork they needed to get a search warrant for the house. They were going to go in later tonight, when the Riveros got back from dinner, but then you and your friends showed up."

"Would have been nice if someone told me about all this."

"How could we? You weren't answering your phone. Besides, we thought you were safer if you didn't know. I should have known better."

"You could have sent a text?"

"Halle . . . ," North grumbled.

"What?"

"Come on, there are a lot of people anxious about finding you. Your sister, Max, dad and mom for starters."

"You're all here?"

"Yeah, we arrived an hour ago. When we couldn't find you on campus, we started to panic. Your dad and Max are up here on the hill with me. Your mom and sister went looking for you in the village. When I saw your two friends come crashing out of the woods, I took off running. The boy just kept yelling you were still back here. I think your dad stopped to question him."

North looked into Halle's wide hazel eyes. "You should never have taken this on yourself." He pressed his forehead to Halle's, his short sandy hair tangling with her now wet long brown tresses.

"No one was listening to me, North. I didn't have proof. And I couldn't leave it alone. Alex's future is depending on me. "

Uncle Mike's voice bounced off the trees surrounding them. "Halle! North! Where are you!"

North inhaled slowly as he dropped his hands from Halle's flushed cheeks. She shivered, missing the warmth of his powerful body as he pulled away.

"Go get him," North said, his voice low.

"Over here, Uncle Mike!"

CHAPTER 68

Halle spotted her uncle, then to his left her father, Max, Izzy, and Wyatt. Thank God.

"Daddy!" she cried, running to him as he tromped through the brush toward her.

He picked her up as soon as they touched, crushing her to his barrel chest. Dropping her to the ground, he inspected her from head to toe for any sign of injury before speaking.

"You scared the crap out of us, Halle!" he said, the look on his face fierce, yet tender, as he picked her up a second time, squeezing her until she gasped for air and tears welled in the corners of her eyes.

Halle pushed against his chest. "Dad, I can't breathe."

"I don't care. I thought I lost you." Graham Henry's graying hair stood on end as he released his bear-like hold, cupping the back of his youngest daughter's head and bringing his cheek, rough with two days' growth, against hers. "I'm serious, Hal. I swear I'm going to stick a tracking chip in your arm if you try something like this again. I'm too old for this."

"I love you too, Daddy," Halle choked out, finally realizing the worry she'd put her family through, again.

"Oh my God, Halle, I was so scared!" Izzy cried, reaching out for her roommate once she was out of her father's arms. "When Wyatt ran out of there alone I didn't know what to do."

Wyatt shuffled his feet next to Izzy. Grabbing him, Halle pulled him into a three-way hug, laughing at the shocked look in his eyes when they embraced.

"You're one of us now, Donley. Get used to it. Friends hug." After a shared minute, Halle released him, gently slugging his shoulder. "I cannot believe you knocked that guy out with a paint can. That was awesome."

Izzy's eyes widened. "What?"

Wyatt chuckled, shoving his hands deep into the front pockets of his muddied tracksuit pants. "Hey, I'm a badass. What can I say?" he said, shrugging.

"Okay, guys," Uncle Mike said, stepping up to the group. "Why don't we take this back down to campus? My men should have the Riveros in custody. As soon as things started happening at the house, we moved in. The school is onboard, and we've set up a makeshift hub at the headmaster's house. Your mom and sister will be there. I'm sure they're anxious to see you, Halle."

"I think I need a Scotch," Graham said, slapping his brother-in-law on the back.

Mike agreed. "Yeah, me too."

North unzipped his jacket and placed the warm coat over Halle's shoulders. "Come on, Hal."

"Lead the way, Uncle Mike."

Grabbing Halle loosely by the neck, Uncle Mike pulled her under his arm. "Kiddo, what on earth are we going to do with you?"

Halle bumped her hip to his. "You could start listening to me when I'm telling you something's wrong next time."

"Next time?"

A sly smile creased Halle's cheeks. "Isn't there always a next time?"

Mike shook his head. "You're killing me."

"I'm teasing you, Uncle Mike."

"Ever think of going into criminal investigation? University of British Columbia has a great program."

Graham stopped. "Oh no you don't, Mike. Hell, no!"

Halle laughed. "Don't worry, Dad. I've got my heart set on an engineering degree from somewhere in the U.K. I want to be closer to you guys."

Graham's shoulders relaxed. "That's my girl."

Behind her, North smiled.

CHAPTER 69

Lili walked the length of the covered porch fronting the headmaster's house. Mr. Smith had graciously allowed the select members of the Tamuran secret service and the respective Canadian law enforcement departments to set up their investigation headquarters over the past hour.

"Mom," Blakely said, stepping alongside Lili, linking their arms together. "Dad just called. They've got Halle and the others, and they're on their way back here."

"Oh, thank God." Lili sighed with relief.

"Dad said the police now have the two men that were in the house and the Riveros in custody."

"So it's over?"

"It's over, Mom."

Blakely kissed Lili's cheek. "They should be here any minute."

When Lili first heard what Halle was doing she was angry, but now all she wanted to do was hold her youngest daughter in her arms and never let go.

The heavy mist left by the rain shrouded Halle and the others from sight as they approached the headmaster's house. The windows of the Tudor-style home glowed warmly behind Lili, and a ribbon of smoke coiled from the top of the brick chimney.

"Mom!" Halle cried, spotting her first and breaking from the group.

Lili turned at the sound of Halle's voice. "Halle!" Lili flew down the front steps, pulling Halle into her arms. "Is everything okay? Let me look at you."

"She's good," Graham assured her. "She's just grounded till the end of time."

"Dad . . ."

"Don't argue with your father," Lili chided, unwilling to let go.

CHAPTER 70

Ramon struggled against the steel cuffs now binding his wrists as a police officer led him through the back door of the Lakeview Academy school kitchen.

The drug enforcement teams stationed outside the Riveros' house made the call to arrest the couple as soon as the children entered the residence.

"Let me go!" Lola screamed, struggling as two officers wrestled to contain her. "This is all your fault, Ramon! You just had to kill Nico, didn't you! I told you we should have run."

"Shut up, woman," Ramon snarled angrily, sending his wife a warning glare as they were shoved into separate squad cars sitting at the kitchen's delivery entrance.

Ramon wondered if they would be extradited to Florida after the Canadian government charged him for murder and drug trafficking. He doubted it.

What would they charge Lola with, aiding and abetting? Regardless, he wouldn't have to hear her high-pitched voice nagging him every time he turned around for some time. The thought almost made him smile, in spite of the situation he currently found himself in.

CHAPTER 71

Dressed in a pair of pressed slacks and a cashmere sweater that matched the brown specks in her green eyes, Mrs. Smith placed a teapot on the center of the round oak table in the breakfast nook. Beige tiled countertops continued a neutral color scheme from the kitchen to the living room while a large island with a butcher block countertop sat opposite the stove.

Her husband hadn't had a night like this since Blakely attended Lakeview. She loved the Henry girls, they were wonderful students and charming young ladies, but secretly she would be thankful when they were no longer in attendance at Lakeview Academy.

Ten people crowded into a space built for six. Halle sat between Lili and Izzy, on the far side, looking back into the cozy kitchen.

The kitchen, abuzz with activity just a short while ago, now vibrated with a different energy: one of relief. The police and the other operatives had moved out, leaving only a handful of lingering secret service agents occupying the headmaster's personal offices.

The Riveros, now known by all as Lola and Ramon Perez, were in the process of being booked, charged with international drug smuggling, money laundering, and the murder of Nico Soto. What was left of his body had finally washed up on a beach near the south side of Gabriola Island that morning, bloated and riddled with crabs.

Halle, Izzy, and Wyatt gripped warm mugs while a pile of dry towels was passed around for all who had been out in the weather to use.

Mr. Smith poured two fingers of twelve-year-old single malt into Graham's cup then his own, asking the other adults in the room if they cared to join in.

"Please don't take this the wrong way, but I'll be happy when I see you walk upon the stage and receive your diploma in a couple months, Halle Henry," the headmaster joked. His thick white eyebrows reminded Halle of a beloved character in a classic movie.

The side door swung open, and Mr. Davies walked in, wearing his customary jacket and tie, stamping his wet boots on the entry mat. Mrs. Smith took his damp trench coat and hung it on the peg by the door to dry. He nodded to Mr. Smith and reintroduced himself to the Henrys, whom he'd met only once during teacher conferences the year he started with the school.

"John." Mr. Smith welcomed him, shaking his hand. "I believe Miss Henry has uncovered some rather substantial evidence she'd like to present you with in regard to our rather harsh treatment of her and especially of Mr. Dumas."

Beneath the table, Izzy squeezed Halle's knee.

"So I've heard," Mr. Davies said, taking a seat.

"Tea?" Mrs. Smith asked.

"No, I believe I'll need a bit of what your husband's partaking in for this one," he said, his right cheek dimpling as Mr. Smith reached for the single malt Scotch.

"Um, Mr. Davies, exactly what have you heard?" Halle squeaked nervously.

"Enough to think you should all have work hours for sneaking off campus."

Halle frowned, slipping lower in her chair.

"I think, however, in light of what you've discovered, and the money you've saved the school, that we could wave punishment this time." His voice remained serious, yet softened slightly. "As long as you all promise not to do anything dangerous for the remainder of the year."

Halle nodded quickly. "Yes, sir. I promise. We all promise."

"Then tell me everything you know involving our young Mr. Dumas."

"Thank you!" Halle said and launched into what Alex had seen on the ferry, followed by the reasons she believed the drugs had been planted in Alex's bag in the first place, confirming Alex's innocence once and for all.

Mr. Davies took a deep breath. He tossed back his glass of Scotch, smiling, his features easing, making him look almost friendly. "I believe I have a call to make and a student to welcome back to campus. If you'll excuse me."

CHAPTER 72

"Oh my God!" Halle moaned, placing a heaping mound of scrambled eggs into her mouth. "This is so good."

"They're scrambled eggs, Hal." North laughed, rolling his eyes.

"No, you don't understand." Halle picked up a sausage lying next to her half-eaten pile of fluffy bright-colored eggs. She'd been dismissed from her morning classes in order to spend time with her family before they left. Halle didn't really want them to leave, but the sooner things got back to normal the better, she decided.

"This, this is real meat, and these," Halle pointed the sausage toward the eggs, "don't taste like rubber."

Blakely laughed from the bench across from Halle, where she sat next to Max in Mason Hall. "It couldn't have been that bad."

"Oh, but it was," Halle insisted, nodding vigorously. For a change of pace, she wore her hair down, the way her dad liked it. A stray, weather-bleached strand stuck to her cheek, which she quickly brushed away with the back of her hand. She itched beneath the gray flannel skirt of her informal school uniform. The rest were all dressed casually for the flight home.

After the Riveros were taken away, the school hired a temporary chef from one of the local restaurants, delighting all on campus.

"Morning," Lili said, approaching the table with a coffee in hand. Halle's parents and Max and North spent the night in Mr. Smith's guest quarters while Blakely slept in Halle's room. "Blakely, Max, North, don't forget to get all your things together. The car taking us to the airport will be here at eleven."

"Already done," said Max.

Lili headed back to the staff table where she and Graham were sitting with several of the faculty not currently teaching, whom they'd come to know over the years.

"You sure you don't want us to stay a little longer, Hal?" Blakely asked.

"No, like I said, I'll see you in just under two months for graduation. Plus Uncle Mike will be in and out of here for the next week getting things wrapped up. I'm good."

"Yeah, I'll bet he'll make sure to listen to you next time you come to him with something," teased Max.

"When does Alex come back?" North asked.

"Tomorrow," Halle said, smiling.

Blakely sucked in a breath between her teeth. "Is he still mad at you?" Last night they talked well past midnight, and Halle told her about what Alex had threatened.

"I don't know. He certainly doesn't seem happy about what we did. But he did say he was glad to be coming back. I'm sure things will be better once we see each other."

Blakely nodded, hoping for her sister's sake they would.

"Think you can stay out of trouble for the next forty days?" said North, blowing the steam from the top of his well-sugared mug of tea.

Halle rolled her eyes. "Yes! Why does everyone keep asking that question?"

"Why do you think?"

"Come on, I'm not that bad."

North smirked, one brow rising above the other. "That's still up for debate."

"Well, nothing better happen. At this point I think Mom will have a heart attack if anything else happens around here," Blakely said, leaning into her fiancé's shoulder. Her diamond ring sparkled in the morning light streaming through the windows of the dining hall.

"Yeah, I got a twenty saying she'll try to blame me for any new wrinkles she finds," Halle said.

Blakely smiled. "You got that right. I love that it's finally you too, and not me for once."

CHAPTER 73

Halle, Wyatt, and Izzy stood by the flagpole at the front of the admissions building the following afternoon. The sun shone brightly, not a cloud in sight, a rare, warm early spring afternoon, the irony of which was not lost on Halle, since the weather matched their moods perfectly. The Canadian flag snapped overhead, the breeze coming off the lake chilling the air around them slightly. Mr. Davies had allowed them to skip their sport practices to welcome Alex back to campus.

A forest-green Explorer rounded the corner and made its way through the winding drive. Halle held her breath. She didn't mean to, she just couldn't help it. Alex sat in the passenger seat, his mom in the back while his dad drove. Halle could swear she could see him smiling, although he was still over a hundred meters away. She closed her eyes, letting the sun warm the lids for a brief second, feeling happier than she had since before Alex had left.

The car slowed and pulled into one of the three parking slips in front of the main academic building. Alex stepped out, and Halle ran to him, throwing her arms around his broad shoulders.

Alex returned the embrace, but his body remained stiff. He was still angry that she had acted on her own and talked Izzy and Wyatt into helping her. He kissed her temple. "Hey."

"Hey yourself." Halle sighed, hugging him tightly, hoping that time would help him forgive her.

The twins' mother stepped out of the car next.

"Mama," Izzy squealed, rushing up to hug her.

Wyatt watched uncomfortably from the curb before accepting a brief bro hug from Alex, who laughed at his squeamish expression.

"Too much emotion for you, dude?" Alex teased, tossing his chin in the girls' direction. His sister welcomed their father while Halle exchanged two cheek kisses with his mother as a greeting.

"Man, I'm just glad you're back. Your girlfriend is a pain in the ass."

Alex laughed through his nose. "Yeah, tell me something I don't know."

"Oh no, Wyatt," Halle said, overhearing their conversation and returning to Alex's side. "You're not starting with that again. We bonded. You used the friend word with me. No sinking back into your old jerk ways now, buddy."

"See what I mean?" Wyatt said, looking from one to the other.

"So, Isabel, where's this boyfriend of yours I've heard so much about," Mrs. Dumas asked, her round cheeks dimpling as she smiled.

Heat flooded Izzy's face, turning it pink. "Alex!" Izzy yelled, accusing her brother of telling their parents her secrets. She hoped to save Jacob from what would surely be the second inquisition if he were forced into meeting her overprotective father.

"Jacob, right? That's his name?" Mr. Dumas asked his daughter.

Izzy glared at her brother. She never brought up her love life around her parents. Especially when she'd been dating less than a month.

Alex smiled, blowing her a kiss.

"Yes, Daddy," Izzy said. "If you like, I can ask him to join us for dinner tonight."

"That would be nice."

Her father might be softer around the middle than he was in his twenties, and balding, but Izzy hated how intimidating he could be when it came to the boys she dated.

Halle twined her fingers through Alex's. The warmth of his hand back in hers made her feel like the nightmare was truly over.

CHAPTER 74

Lakeview Academy

June

Two white tents were set up on the formal lawns, shading guests from the sun's intense glare. A podium stood on the stage dressed in elaborate floral bouquets.

Halle eased the collar of her formal uniform, feeling abnormally warm. She wondered if anyone ever died from having to wear a blazer and tie in thirty-one-plus degrees Celsius. She did the conversion in her head: eighty-nine degrees. No wonder she felt like she was melting.

In the rows of chairs surrounding Halle sat her classmates. Because her last name started with *H*, she sat in the middle of the student tent, on the aisle. Alex and Izzy sat next to Wyatt, in the row with the rest of the students whose names began with the letter *D*.

Mr. Davies surprised Alex a couple days after his arrival back on campus when he called him into his office for the second time that year and told him he had personally contacted the dean of admissions at the University of Washington, Alex's first choice.

Since Alex never let his grades drop during his absence, and bounced back to lead the Lakeview rowing team to victory at the provincial championships in May, the dean revisited his application, happily extending a full scholarship for Alex to row for the UW in the fall.

Halle's eyes started to water. She tried to pull the moisture back in but it was no use. The damn things wouldn't listen. She couldn't believe this was it. The end. After today, there would be no more Lakeview. She swiped her eyes, hoping no one else saw, then spotted several of her classmates doing the same thing. Something about this place got under her skin. She'd been around the campus for ten of her eighteen years, counting the times she'd visited while her sister attended.

Halle let her gaze float through the rows of families, spotting her mom, dad, aunt, uncle, Blakely, and Max. Even several of the Tamuran officials, whom she'd grown close to after their family moved into the castle, came to see her graduate, Lord Girard and his new wife, Annabelle, among them. North couldn't make it, as he'd qualified to tour New Zealand with his rugby club for the month of June. Instead, he sent her a card attached to the most beautiful bouquet of pink roses she'd ever seen.

She could still barely believe that Max would be her brother-in-law soon. She couldn't wait. He and Blakely were going to have an awesome life together. They were so in love. The wedding plans were well underway. They had decided on a date, September 19, three weeks before the start of her first term at Oxford. She found out about her acceptance the day after Alex returned to school. Izzy, on the other hand, decided to go to NYU, where she would study fashion. Her parents agreed to let her spend the summer in Tamura with Halle, so they would be flying back together after the graduation parties concluded on Monday.

Halle wondered if she would ever find a match like Max. Things between her and Alex were never quite the same after he returned to campus. Although she felt proud of herself for helping him, Alex never completely forgave her for putting herself at risk, and the stress it caused created a rift in their relationship that Halle didn't know how to fix. They made it to the end of the year, though, before deciding to go their separate ways after school ended. Her heart physically ached at the thought of life without him. It sucked. He would always be her first love, and for that, she was truly grateful.

Halle found his head in the rows in front of her, his mound of wavy black hair neatly combed for once, easy to find, as it sat well above the rest. She wondered what he was feeling, if he struggled to choke back his emotions as well. At least they got to say their goodbyes properly this time.

The commencement speaker finished wishing the graduating class good luck in their future endeavors. Halle could hear birds chirping as they chased the bugs that skimmed the reeds at the lake's edge. A shiver ran down her spine. The students' names were being read one after the other. She watched as her friends were called in alphabetical order, and they stepped upon the stage in front of her.

"Julia Finch," the headmaster read. "Three years, Windsor House. Julia will be heading to McGill University.

"Andrew Gallagher, two years, Burns House, Captain boys' soccer. Andrew will be attending Middlebury College.

"Halle Henry . . ."

Halle stood, straightened her shoulders, and walked down the aisle.

Thank you for reading *Scream,* the third book in the Lakeview Novel series!

If you enjoyed it, please let me know.

Review it on **Amazon** and/or on **Goodreads** today.

I can't do what I do without you.

Connect with Stacey R. Campbell to find out what else is going on at Lakeview Academy:

AUTHOR WEBSITE
www.staceyrcampbell.com

TWITTER
@staceyrcampbell

YOUTUBE
Stacey R. Campbell

FACEBOOK
Authorstaceyrcampbell

BOOKS BY STACEY R. CAMPBELL

THE LAKEVIEW NOVEL SERIES

Hush

Whisper

Scream

Silence (Summer, 2015)

Bliss (Winter, 2015)

OTHER BOOKS BY STACEY R. CAMPBELL

ARRGH!

Sock Monster (Fall, 2015)

ACKNOWLEDGMENTS

Acknowledgments are always the hardest thing to write. So many people contribute to the publication of a book, and I am always afraid I am going to forget someone and look like a putz.

Writing is not a glamorous job. Sometimes that walk with your good friend, on a day you don't want to acknowledge your keyboard, can turn into a life-saving plot twist. Texting an image can turn into a book cover, and asking for advice can save your sanity. Thank you Anna M., Christie J., Diana A., and Kristie R. for being all that and so much more.

Hannah W. & Jessica B., you are amazing beta readers. Your work and comments helped make this book all that and more.

Mike R., you rock. Thanks for all the great police info. I love that you're in this book.

Kari Hock, my wonderful and talented publisher, thank you so very much for taking a chance on me. Here's to our fourth project together—*clink*! You really do make dreams come true.

Sally Carr, editor extraordinaire, I swear you know what I'm going to say and write before I do. It completely freaks me out, ha-ha. I am so grateful for your patience and hard work!

Jason Enterline, your covers rock! Thank you for making my books look so darn good!

Judy and Dad, you are my biggest cheerleaders; words will never be enough to tell you how appreciative I am for all your support.

Blakely, Leigh, and Halle, none of this would be possible without you. You are my first readers, my inspiration, and the very reason I write. I love you girls so much. I am the luckiest mother in the world. And Donald, my partner of more than twenty-five years, you are always the last to read my books, but you are always the first to believe in what

I've written, even when you've never seen the words I've typed. Your unending devotion to me, and my various and often random passions, floors me. You might not do everything I ask, but you are everything I need.

Friends, readers, bloggers, librarians, and booksellers, you inspire me daily. Without your constant, humbling, and jaw-dropping support I wouldn't be where I am today. You make a little dyslexic girl who was told she would never be a writer feel like she's walking on cloud nine. I am so excited to share my stories with all of you. I just wish there were more hours in the day so I could get all of them to you sooner.

Thank you all and remember always: dreams do come true!

ABOUT STACEY R. CAMPBELL

Stacey R. Campbell lives in the San Juan Islands with her husband and three daughters. She is a graduate of the University of Washington and a dyslexic writer who believes there is no such thing as a bad reader. She is the author of the young adult novels **Hush** and **Whisper**, and the highly acclaimed middle grade swashbuckling pirate book **ARRGH!**

When not at her desk writing she can be found hiking, sailing, or skiing. She enjoys chocolate in any shape or size, too many cups of coffee, and laughing (often too loudly, as her daughters say) with her friends and family.

Stacey is available for classroom visits and loves working with writers and readers of any age, especially those with learning disabilities like her own.

For more information please contact Green Darner Press at www.greendarnerpress.com.

CPSIA information can be obtained
at www.ICGtesting.com
Printed in the USA
FSOW01n1419300715
9295FS